CAMOUFLAGE

NATASHA WHITE

authorHOUSE®

AuthorHouse™ UK Ltd.
1663 Liberty Drive
Bloomington, IN 47403 USA
www.authorhouse.co.uk
Phone: 0800.197.4150

*This is a work of fiction. All of the characters, names, incidents, organizations, and dialogue
in this novel are either the products of the author's imagination or are used fictitiously.*

Published by AuthorHouse   06/02/2014

ISBN: 978-1-4969-8257-5 (sc)
ISBN: 978-1-4969-8256-8 (hc)
ISBN: 978-1-4969-8255-1 (e)

*Any people depicted in stock imagery provided by Thinkstock are models,
and such images are being used for illustrative purposes only.
Certain stock imagery* © *Thinkstock.*

This book is printed on acid-free paper.

"*You'll be shocked from the very first page, and that's a good thing. Natasha is a breath of terrifying fresh air in new Irish fiction, not since reading "may we be forgiven" by A.M.Homes have I been as thrown immediately, into the deep end by a book, and wanted to stay there.*"

Doodle Kennelly, journalist, Sunday Independent, and author of "I'm doing my best", her Autobiography.

"To the people who know me best, may my character stay fictional!
I dedicate "Sophie" to the many women who've daydreamed
about having the upper hand, revenge or retribution, may her
actions give you joy, she would be my alter ego. To my children,
I apologise for depriving you of attention while I stared into
space thinking murderous thoughts, and of course my one and
only – Spud, for encouraging me to finally get this done"

"Sometimes the scariest things in life are

those we dismiss as ordinary"

PREFACE

I chose to write this out of frustration, where are all the female serial killers I asked? Seems the only ones I've heard about were abused, tortured, driven to the edge, and from the USA. So I asked myself—is it possible for a normal girl in Ireland to be a killer and yet blend in, and the answer – hypothetically—is yes. If nature and nurture play no part in forming a killer, who or what do you blame? It's also my massive two fingers to "Chick Lit"

I've taken the liberty of referring to murders and real disappearances in Ireland in recent years as part of the story and in doing so I hope I haven't offended anyone. The characters are fictional and not, I might add, based on anyone I know, though some are shadowy past encounters. So, if you see yourself as any of the characters mentioned you're being narcissistic. I have drawn on childhood memories but twisted them for the purpose of fiction.

My interest in murder and serial killers dates back to my teens, and perhaps in a different life, I could have been a Sophie. I wish to thank anyone in law enforcement for keeping us all safe from the real life terrors, and having more intelligence than my character would give credit.

While, like my character, I have studied various methods of killing and disposal, I'm quite proud that I haven't actually killed anyone-yet.

I've tried to keep the locations mentioned as true to life as possible, and all are real places in Dublin and Wicklow.

CHAPTER 1

There's nothing like a recession to screw up ambitions of climbing the corporate ladder, and nothing like the fear of losing a well paid job to make a girl dig her claws into its greasy rungs.

Six months had passed under the critical eye of her new boss, he was starting to give off signs of fatigue, there was no doubt in her abilities; she was good at her job but not exceptional at the moment thanks to the downturn in the economy.

Her work was faultless, and her relationship with the company's clients was without a hitch. Sophie put in the effort required just like other aspects of her life where her planning and execution were faultless. But this guy was becoming hard to please and he was demanding higher, unachievable targets. Her previous and hard won reputation as a "go-getter" was fading, fast.

Sophie had jumped into this position by sleeping with her previous boss, a sixty something, easily flattered and unappreciated corporate robot on a slow countdown to retirement and replacement. Jesus, it was ridiculous how easily he was swayed by her attentions; he never had a chance to see the honey trap coming.

In the fast moving world of PR the guy was a dinosaur, constantly left behind by younger, more aggressive and ruthless colleagues, his childhood friendship with the boss Dave Duffy the only thing keeping him from the corporate chopping block. Thankfully, he had died of a massive coronary on the 6th hole of the exclusive K-Club golf course, so his indiscretions went to the grave with him, lucky for him, and even luckier for the unsuspecting and grieving widow he left behind; still, she was left with unsullied memories and a big fat life insurance policy. But Sophie's job security had died with the bastard.

The only thing she had inherited was a hit and miss client list and a demanding asshole of a new boss. Life under the old guy had been easier in every respect.

Now she was watching her colleagues and team leaders being whittled down to only the most ruthless in the firm. A company which, during the Celtic tiger boom, had held the position of top performing P.R. and marketing beast in the Irish economy, top of their game. At one stage she had twenty cock sure and aggressive sales executives she could set on clients, now, just a few remained.

Each colleague was as eager as the next to impress, selling their souls for the next big contract. During the building boom of the Celtic tiger years Sophie had the luxury of turning away business, now it was a scramble to gather the crumbs.

It was becoming harder and harder to motivate them to meet her spiraling targets. Even the battle hardened executives were feeling the pressure and the cream of the crop had already left, taking their reputation and ability to close deals with them. She was left with a revolving door of short lived amateurs, nervous, inexperienced, but willing to please none the less.

At least she had built up a network of reliable and successful clients, religiously looking up their annual accounts on the Companies registration office, and it gave her an insight into the longevity of their business. In Irish business you never took someone's word; it was a case of money talks, bullshit walks, always.

Too many of her colleagues had poured time and effort into promotional campaigns for companies on the ropes, trying to resurrect them, only to find their invoices going unpaid; and their job under threat as a result. She wasn't going to make that mistake. Her contacts reached far into the Irish media, radio, TV and newspapers, it allowed her to keep a finger on the pulse and hear whatever juicy gossip and scandal was too libelous to publish. She picked through it and used some of the inside information to her advantage, to keep ahead of the herd.

There was no question of her having to stoop to the lows of sleeping with clients for business, sure, some clients had flirted with her, had dangled the carrot of business over her, but she could back up her fees with results instead of short term gratification and a quick fumble in the car park. Pity her new boss didn't appreciate that.

She had worked long hours during the boom, travelled to the far flung corners of Ireland for a ten minute meeting but she always made time for her own "outside" interests. No way was work going to swallow her up and deprive her of the leisure activities she enjoyed.

She watched some of the women in 'Duffy PR' and how they conducted themselves; they were loud, brazen, and slept around as much as the men in the firm. They guzzled down the cheap, nasty wine at every launch, eager as whores to feature in each press photo. No way was she lowering her standards to behave like that. She walked the fine line between aloof and amiable. She wasn't going to whore herself again. Her parents had raised her to appreciate hard work and subsequent reward; it stood her well in all aspects of her life. Her sleeping with the old boss had been a necessary evil at the time, it wasn't her finest moment, and at least nobody within the company had any suspicions.

Sophie had what could be considered a well behaved and unremarkable schooling, courtesy of the convent school run by, what seemed an entire order of sadist nuns and lesbians in denial; it was an expensive education in South Dublin. She had excelled in the leaving but spurned medicine on her CAO forms, much to the disappointment of her two GP parents.

They were career conscious but well intentioned parents, her father enjoying a leisurely retirement, enjoying new hobbies and making friends, while her mother still clung to the remains of her career as an on-call locum. So, they poured their efforts into her sister Charlotte instead, much to Sophie's relief, allowing her to indulge in what they considered to be a useless business degree.

Despite of the lack of parental interference and over bearing guidance she had done pretty well for herself. She was only twenty five, held a business degree and an executive position normally reserved for the Forty—plus brigade. It would generally have taken a good twenty years of groveling, ass kissing and stomach ulcers to get her job, but she was an Alpha female in camouflage. She enjoyed watching the herd of co—workers file in every morning knowing that her brains and ability had elevated her without too much sacrifice, but she still had a bit to go to break the glass ceiling in the company.

The surprising thing was that her co-workers and subordinates liked her, they didn't begrudge her the success, she could easily listen to the female "Boo—Hoo" stories of broken hearts and bastard boyfriends at the coffee machine, she allowed the guys their risqué jokes without showing offence or laughing out loud like a slut, but these people didn't know her, no —one really knew Sophie, because if they did they'd have been very uncomfortable.

She kept in touch with old school friends through Facebook and occasional lunch dates, allowing the others to steer the conversation. They were mostly married with kids; none had the bottle to emigrate, instead choosing a punishing mortgage and crap weather just to stay close to home. Fear of the unknown was a common threat to Irish success. Her friends rewarded themselves with yearly package holidays with kids clubs just to keep their sanity.

Facebook was her main way of keeping in touch with people; she chose that rather than having to endure long winded conversations. She never took her mobile with her when she went out for "after work" activities, for good reason.

Sophie never allowed anyone get too close to her, she was that human anomaly that's nice to everyone, everyone likes her and greets her like a long lost friend, kind words here and there, a joke shared, a promised lunch date. Conversations were always light and easy and ended with much smiling, hugs and cheek kissing. But, if you ever asked yourself — did I learn anything about her in that conversation? the answer would inevitably be a big fat no, but no—one ever pondered that question.

To her colleagues she was a nice girl who had done well for herself without being flash, she never dressed provocatively, yet never dowdy, clothes just seemed to fit her form effortlessly but she hadn't crossed that female battle line where admiration turned to jealousy, she appeared successful but non—threatening. Yet when she washed off the bland, unflattering, work day makeup, discarded the suit, took away the harsh and unfashionable glasses, let down the pony tail of expensively maintained and natural blonde hair she became a different animal in all respects, she was stunning but very well camouflaged from nine to five.

Had they known what her other compulsions and motivations were they'd have a great story to tell their mates.

She had often wondered if she was betraying the people around her with her persona, she knew she had a dark side, then again, most highly competent professionals did. The only time her well hidden aggression showed its ugly face was outside the office in situations she orchestrated and controlled. To all in the office Sophie Murphy was just a normal hard working, considerate girl. She intended keeping it that way. Everything depended on her tailor made mask.

CHAPTER 2

Two hours was her absolute minimum in the gym most evenings, it was here she could take out all her rage and pent up frustrations on the array of machines in the overpriced poseurs gym. If she had a particularly bad day she could always beat the shit out of the boxing bag.

She was way beyond the average female "gym Bunny" fitness level; she wasn't here to pose in the multitude of deliberately flattering mirrors or trot on a treadmill while watching "Eastenders" on the overhead screens. She took this seriously and besides, she needed strength and stamina for some of the things that occupied her "other" life. She never spoke to anyone, avoided making eye contact, or getting caught up in idle chatter, her MP3 stayed on full volume for the duration of her work outs.

She assaulted her eardrums with the most aggressive and bitter music America could throw up. She could wow any depressed, parent hating, EMO teenager with her knowledge of heavy metal but the music didn't impress her, it served a purpose, kept her focused, pumped and aggressive while training, like everything in her life it served a purpose and there was no sentiment attached.

This evening she was pushing herself hard. The cardio was taking its toll and beads of sweat steadily trickled from her armpits and traced its way down tickling her ribs. Her temples and hairline were soaking but she was savoring the feeling of pushing herself like this, beating her feet down on the running machine with extra venom, grabbing the rail to increase the speed and incline, she could feel the familiar burn in her calves rising, it was only when she reached the end of her strength that she could uncoil her physical and mental being, like a penitent who craves the sting of the lash, this treadmill was her cat of nine tails. Opus Dei would have been proud of her but she didn't subscribe to that or any other religious bullshit, despite the schools nun's best efforts at ramming it down her throat.

She lingered in the lobster boiling shower, turning to let the water pummel her aching muscles, her hair fell like a blonde waterfall over her flushed face, she ignored all around her, her mind busy pondering the problem this new boss presented. This guy was a different breed of mature man to his predecessor or predeceased — the play on words amused her, and she turned her smirk into the hot beating water. This guy was not going to fall for flattery and seduction, he was old school and he was going to be a challenge. This was novel to Sophie but also worrying, if she fucked this up not only was her job gone, but so was the apartment, car and financial freedom she'd become accustomed to. She didn't find men a challenge at all, once you pressed the right buttons, massaged the ego, became who they wanted you to be — or who their wife wasn't, she could become their fantasy female and they in turn became her playthings and benefactors, her contemptuous, childish, pathetic playthings to be used and discarded once they served their purpose.

This new challenge was risky, if she played this one wrong her world would fall apart, this had never been a risk factor before, but shit, she was not about to let that happen. She was expert at being careful and very discreet; she could mask her venomous side, keep her head down and study him. A good hunter always studies the terrain and by god was she a good hunter.

The crosshairs in her mind worked through what she knew of him privately, his children, where he lived, his previous employment. Then it struck her, a novel way to deal with him and keep him in check, a real life Trojan horse, infiltrate his family life in the most despicable way possible, she decided to seduce his wife.

At the back of the gym car park her BMW sat shinning among the common dross of commuter belt cars and mammy wagons. She slid into the leather seat, punched the CD button, volume up full, and lit a cigarette before gunning it out onto the main road. She had that feel good buzz from the exercise and because now she had focus, a plan, which meant only one more thing was required tonight, she wanted to fuck. she hit speed dial knowing this call would be answered, this guy never turned her down, he found her irresistible, insatiable and he loved it, he proved a reliable fuck buddy — for now.

Sophie threaded the car up the dark forested lane, the wide tyres on the BMW easily tackling the rutted gravel that led to the scenic "Three rock" and waited, she wasn't here to admire the glittering city lights spread out below in a hazy panorama, she sat chain smoking in damp anticipation until she saw the headlights round the last clump of trees, a quick flash of high beam — it was him. She slipped out of her warm car and crossed the gravel knowing that in ten minutes she would have the relief she craved.

Sex was not something she experienced like most women, it wasn't the touchy feely intimate experience she knew other women enjoyed and spent a lifetime craving and trying to recreate. If violence or force didn't come into play she became bored. If a guy didn't thrust hard enough, or squeeze her throat just a little bit she found it bland and boring. This new shag buddy was pressing all the right buttons for her, her scalp often stung from his over enthusiasm with her blonde ponytail. She knew that things could turn dangerous; he was a notorious drug dealer. He surrounded himself with hard men in the background and dolly-bird models in the limelight of the Dublin social scene. To look at him you could be fooled into thinking Justin Mulholland was a well heeled executive, he drove an understated but powerful car, wore suits from bespoke Dublin tailor Louis Copeland. He was a south Dublin boy from the right side of the tracks who chose a shady career, he was well known to the inner circle of socialites, and was regularly seen sipping champagne in nightclubs with only the most popular young PR girls, actresses and models. Like Sophie he used camouflage, though his mask was of respectable businesses to conceal his real income generator. His mother and Barrister father often bragged to their peers on the golf course about "their Justin" and his latest entrepreneurial success. The recession was seemingly leaving him unaffected, unusual, given the havoc the "green" government and economy had wreaked on the motor industry. In fact, his business was thriving.

Justin had succeeded so far, in cultivating a lifestyle that involved rubbing shoulders with models, minor celebrities and the sons and daughters of Dublin's wealthy elite. He managed to keep far enough under the radar to avoid attracting the searching gaze of the drugs squad and Criminal assets bureau. He was one of the biggest importers of coke and dope in Ireland but this was not common knowledge to anyone in authority. He paid his V.A.T. bills on time to the nonchalance of the Revenue Commissioners; so for all intents and purposes, he was as respectable and trustworthy as the second hand cars his salesmen sold from a small, neat forecourt off the main city artery of the Naas road. He was always careful to employ well spoken, groomed and handsome young guys to man the forecourt, no working class, thick city accented "Howiya's" as he called them. However, if you chose to look carefully at his entourage and those he whispered to in night club corners, the veneer of respectability began to tarnish and chip away, only to reveal a subculture and alternative lifestyle that most people only read about in the Sunday papers and would hopefully never encounter.

Justin's other lifestyle and choice of business was not for the faint hearted, But Sophie knew who he was, she was impressed by his D4 accent, tall dark rugby player frame, his Colin Farrell looks made him stand out from the average Irish guy. She had made a bee-line for him in "Reynard's" night club six months before, He could give her what she needed, and what she wanted was Rohypnol among other things, to help someone sleep— but not her. A bond and understanding had been formed which intrigued him and secured a regular supply of anesthetic and illegal drugs for her purposes.

She had met some of his business associates on nights out, they were far removed from the two dimensional characters portrayed on Irish TV. The public had been spoon fed acceptable gangsters courtesy of shows like "Fair City" and "Love/Hate". The "real deal" was not so pleasant. They had an aura of evil about them and she had heard enough stories from Justin to know these guys were to be avoided. They were in league with every known criminal group ranging from the Irish Traveler gangs to the new phenomenon of Eastern European and ex soviet bloc crime gangs. They had a hold of most large towns in Ireland, indulging in criminal activity from prostitution, drugs and protection rackets. Irelands open border policy had opened the floodgates to a new brand of highly organised and violent criminal, taking full advantage our lax criminal justice system and stretched Garda resources. They were gorging themselves on the naivety and inadequacy of Ireland. Justin had recently got in bed with one of the lesser known Latvian gangs who specialised in ringing cars and stealing high power motors to order. All he had to do was tip them off as to the address of the owner, easy cash for Justin, and unfortunate for the poor bastard coming down to breakfast and finding his pride and joy missing from the driveway, by the time the sucker phoned the Gardai his car was either stripped down in a some lock up for parts, or in a container heading for Latvia. Justin earned hefty cash commissions and also had the pleasure of repeat business by replacing the poor guys' car. His business was lucrative on every level.

Meeting Justin had been a stroke of luck, before him she had been forced to rob the occasional prescription pad from her parents' medical bags, but since her father retired and her mother was reducing her workload, it wasn't a situation that could continue. Her mother's old medical reference books had proven invaluable when choosing sedatives, so much for her taking them to the book recycling; they sat proudly on her shelf in the apartment, ready to be thumbed through with a glass of wine and a Chinese take away.

At the security gate of her D4 apartment complex she leaned out of the car window, squinted her eyes, so the smoke from her cigarette glued to her lip gloss wouldn't blind her, and punched in the code. The BMW blended well in this enclave for the successful, she swung into her underground parking space, and made for the private lift to her penthouse apartment, this lift gave her privacy, and was only shared with one other apartment which was thankfully vacant due to the poor bastard losing his job. All the expensive CCTV equipment lay idle, the eyes of the camera's blank and unused due to the builder running out of funds to finish the complex.

She slipped the key in the door and bumped it open with her hip, the subdued glint of chrome and glass was the only relief in the dark. Modern, clean and functional, that was how she liked to have her living space. Most would call it cold, Spartan or masculine.

Sophie didn't bother with the lights, she knew the layout in the dark intimately — she needed to. Dumping her gym bag she half snarled at the repugnant damp feeling in her expensive lingerie and the faint musky odor creeping up inside the front of her T— shirt, this residue of sex she despised.

The shower ran to scalding as she disinfected herself with expensive soap from Italy, threw her lingerie and gym gear in the washing machine and set the TV to record "Dexter" before slipping between the Egyptian cotton sheets and drifted off to what she hoped would be a productive sleep.

In her dreams she was a child again, just her and her dad, parading around Dun Laoghaire on a Saturday, animated conversations with the staff of "Hicks" family butchers, her father joking that they were on a mission to bring home the compulsory "pound of sausages". Buying the obligatory coffee cake from the "Tea Time Express" shop for her mother, the red and gold box carefully tethered with expertly tied gold string, courtesy of the nimble fingered and friendly women behind the counter of delights, then a quick diversion along the coast road to "The Dalkey Island Hotel" for a sneaky pint of Bass for her father, and a fizzy orange for her. The last diversion was always their secret, she never told her mother, even though she was aching to. Frothy, storm blown waves crashed against the conservatory windows in winter, blotting out the island and lighthouse beyond, while a blind man played music in the bar, her feet sinking into the heavy shag carpet under the watchful eyes of suits of armor, everyone there cocooned in its warmth and shelter. Her dreams always brought her back to innocent times, blocking the horrors of more recent life events, she always awoke refreshed after nostalgic dreaming.

CHAPTER 3

The following night however, her dreams were tortured with images of lesbian sex. It wasn't something that disgusted her, she had been with plenty of women but she despised the tenderness involved in their lovemaking.

That was it — the word love, it held no meaning for her, all relationships were simply physical acts, and love was as illusive to her as Santa Claus or the Easter bunny, in her mind love didn't exist, she could explain it away by rationalizing it as a state of mind, a chemical reaction, a duty of care, whatever – it was bullshit.

Sophie's lot in life was to be soul—less without feeling deprived and yet others found her caring and deep. She would use that mask to get to her target, her boss was married to a straight laced mother of two grown up sons from Foxrock and this was going to be the sexual challenge of her life to turn this woman, but what a challenge. She sat unobtrusively eating her breakfast in the staff canteen until her ears were assaulted; she became aware of the giddy female voices invading her private space. She tried to block it out and look as though the property section of "The Times" had her full concentration until her name being screeched shattered the illusion. She didn't need this, she was tired and grumpy from lack of decent sleep but she had mastered the art of keeping up appearances.

She always hated being around excitable women, hysterical, giddy shrill voices always too many octaves too high. It was like nails down a blackboard. Shit, they were waving her over; she feigned daydreaming, stood up and gingerly walked over to the pack of women.

"Sue's pregnant, isn't that great?" mused one of the coven of laughing hyenas.

So, cocking her head to the side and reaching out to hug Sue, she made a wonderful job of congratulating her but if the truth be told — she found the idea of being pregnant revolting, the loss of control, the parasitic invasion of your body, demanding of it, changing your form, she felt bitter bile rising in the back of her throat and yet she could look Sue from the admin department dead in the eye and say "ah Sue, I'm delighted for you, god, maybe someday I'll meet someone nice and get to feel like you today" and Sue being the genuine sort could only reply in innocence "ah thanks, and you will, sure you're a lovely girl, your turn will come, you wait and see". To Sophie this was twisted in her interpretation as a gloating "one up-manship" remark,

twisted in her interpretation as a gloating "one up-manship" remark, her logic was so convoluted and bent that although outwardly she was smiling and breaking out the crocodile tears in happiness for Sue; she was inwardly cooking up visions of beating Sue's head off various items of furniture for gloating at her.

With a cheery wave she snatched up her handbag, trudged to her office sucking her teeth with bitterness and only smiling when she encountered other people.

Sophie was raging inside but she was a master at covering that rage, she excelled in self control, nobody guessed just how homicidal her thoughts were towards Sue and her unborn child at this moment and for that it was a small mercy.

She perceived women with children as smug; the pregnant as physically deformed and avoided dealing with either where possible. She chose late night shopping in the hope of avoiding both.

The scary thing was she was the first to coo over a new baby or hitch a toddler onto her hip if the situation demanded it of her. It seemed her friends were perpetually pregnant or fussing over a new baby. She was always the first to offer congratulations, arrive with presents and sniff and coo over the newborn. She had watched her coworkers return after a lengthy maternity leave, flustered, excited, anxious and distracted. When the initial congratulations wore off they showed themselves to be less competent than before. They had lost that aggressive streak Sophie felt was needed, and she had lost count of the times these women vanished from the office if one of their darlings had a sniffle, or the babysitter let them down.

If she had her way she wouldn't employ them now they were parents, these easily distracted new parents, forever delayed due to crèche drop offs and unreliable minders, refusing the late nights and weekend meetings. Sophie felt they were taking advantage and cheating their barren co workers. While she fevered away at her desk putting together presentations; she was constantly aware in her peripheral vision of some baby photo or video clip on a phone being passed around for approval and praise. Each new parenting achievement distracting them from the job at hand and putting her targets at risk.

Sabotage was the order of the day if she was to gain any kind of insight into her boss's personal life. At least that was her reasoning as she dribbled water from the paper cup into the back of her PC monitor. If her computer was out of action she could use his, along with it the opportunity to intercept calls and make her introduction to the wife when she calls.

The inefficiency of the company's IT staff was legendary so she knew it would be at least tomorrow before the monitor was replaced, a full eight hours in his office to start weaving the web and researching her prey.

Lucky for her corporate golf days for managers were still in vogue, despite the recession, even following the mishap of her previous boss. She even prayed for a repeat of the golf course heart attack, but not even Sophie was that lucky. No, she resigned herself to putting in the graft on this one, and it would be hard work.

The fact that the woman wasn't physically attractive didn't bother Sophie; she could make anyone feel like a supermodel or a stud. This was a means to an end, a project. She would get no physical satisfaction from this farce, but she was an expert at giving pleasure, all she needed was the opportunity, and as luck would have it, her introduction to her prey would come sooner than expected.

She slid behind the walnut desk and surveyed the framed pictures of the two precious sons, non—descript rugby playing types, posh Dublin stereotypes. Just behind the monitor sat a smaller frame with the glorious and well padded jowls of a pampered housewife complete with perma-tan and fake smile for the camera, chubby chin cocked at an awkward, arrogant angle.

An ageing socialite, a falling star, this may not be too hard after all. Then again, she could be a spitting cobra or an innocuous earthworm full of gin and valium, time would tell.

She had encountered plenty of wives like this; successful husbands allowed them to become fat and lazy, their only concern the location of the next holiday. Women like her treated their husbands like ATM's.

Women like this had gone from trophy wives to ungrateful vampires sucking at the husband's wallet, his will to live, and little else that he would have appreciated.

CHAPTER 4

Most Sundays, regardless of the night before or other commitments, Sophie was expected without fail, to lunch at her parent's comfortable suburban home in South Dublin. This Sunday was no exception. It was her parents' way of keeping tabs on their offspring and their opportunity to criticise or guide decisions they were making. Yet Sophie turned up most Sundays with a bouquet for her mother and a kiss on the cheek for her father.

She marveled at the aging process taking place in her parents, there was no pity, just a chance to study the process of slow decline, the way a spider contemplates a fly stuck in its web.

Gone were the angular curves she remembered of her mothers' youth to be replaced by a fleshy roundness and a blurring of her silhouette to a more rounded middle aged form. The waist length blonde hair she remembered had been replaced by a harsh mid brown bob. Her father was grey and running to bald, he was fleshy but embracing middle age instead of fighting it like her mother; he wore the lines on his face well where Sophie's mother — even though she was a GP, regularly treated herself to Botox, and the irony of a doctor injecting herself with poison was not lost on Sophie.

The conversation of work with her mother inevitably reared its head and progress reports were given like exam results for correction. But when Sophie mentioned her new boss, looks were exchanged between her parents, it transpired that Sophie's mum was her GP, but because it was a conversation at the dinner table it was ok to let Sophie in on the fact that the woman had serious problems, she ate valium like "Smarties" and Sophie's mum had been to school with Greta and felt sorry for her. The woman had been such a high flier according to her mother, a glamorous career as an Aer Lingus Stewardess, flying to all the exotic locations imaginable while her peers were up to their eyes in terry toweling nappies and stinking buckets of Milton solution. Though from her mother's passive aggressive bitching it sounded like this woman had hit the skids and was in the throes of a middle aged drink fest.

Now her target had a name — Greta, and a viable connection that could be used.

Sophie spent the rest of the lunch in a daydream concocting scenarios and ways to manipulate this woman and her husband. Her parents had always accused her of daydreaming; perhaps they should have asked her what she was daydreaming about.

Charlotte as usual, was more interested in trying to get Sophie to arrange free tickets for some event or other, no matter how many times it was explained to her that perks and freebies were gone, it still didn't stop her pestering Sophie. Her sister was only too aware of the contacts in media that Sophie used, and the only way to shut her up and move on from the badgering was to promise to blag some concert tickets for her. It amazed Sophie that even when she did come up with the goods, there was never a thank you.

Charlotte could easily afford tickets for any event in D̶ but she had that mean streak which allowed her to have the b̶ ̶ck to expect it for free. What was the point in having a sister with all these media contacts if she couldn't get you free concert tickets or other goodies?

CHAPTER 5

Watery autumn light woke her early the next morning, and she slipped easily into her black Lycra running gear and baseball cap.

The September morning gave little respite from the dark in her apartment and the sole illumination in the pitch dark of the kitchen was from the huge American fridge, she reached into the chrome hulk and took a number of large Tupperware boxes filled with plastic sandwich bags, each packed with meat and bone. She shoved them deep into a black backpack, swung the pack onto her shoulder and headed out towards her lift.

It really felt like Dublin was trapped in an early winter, it was cold, damp, and the air carried the musty wet leaf smell you can still get in a city with old trees before the traffic builds up, even the fleeting sun light fingering through the trees gave no heat. Her breath clouded around her in a misty fog of early morning autumnal chill.

Her apartment complex blended into the stalled skyline dotted with idle cranes, a shameful sign of the property crash.

A mile down the road stood a half finished apartment complex, the hoarding looking shabby, sun bleached and fragile, fraying billboards peeling like discarded snakeskin boasted of "luxury living", the once vivid print now a patchy, peeling water colour. It seemed like a bad joke; and ironic that her PR Company had handled the advertising before the developer went bust. It was just another unfinished cash cow in the clutches of NAMA — the Irish government's version of debt collection for the banks in trouble. Since the recession had bitten and locked its jaws on the economy this was just one of many projects that hadn't made it across the finish line.

Sophie held a steady trot along the length of the hoarding and screening which saved the Dublin residents from being offended by the rotting shell of this failure.

She reached the gap in the fencing at a large padlocked double gate. Inside was an abandoned and fire damaged security hut and above the gates were disconnected and smashed security cameras, obviously a cheaper method of securing the site had been found.

She made a clicking noise and a light whistle to attract the dogs and dropped her backpack at her feet, she checked for traffic and early morning joggers and tipped the meat and bones at the base of the gates, she took a baby-wipe from the packet in her backpack and lay it across the toe of her trainer, then gently nudged the flesh under the gate to the two ravenous and scruffy German Shepherds, both nuzzling at the gap, vicious animals, fur matted into dreadlocks from neglect, barging and snapping at each other in anticipation of the meat. It always amazed her how dogs returned to their feral, wolf like state when hungry. Even the most hardened thieves wouldn't break in here for a haul of copper piping and scrap metal. Within seconds the starving dogs had removed all trace of the meat and had carried off the bones back to a dark, rank corner that should have been the luxurious and concierge manned reception area. Sophie smiled, and used the baby wipe to gather up the blood soaked bags and Tupperware and put them in a nearby litter bin.

The birds had just begun their dawn chorus as she jogged home smiling, the backpack a few pounds lighter. Sophie considered sites like this to be a blessing, In Dublin there were a number of similar developments guarded by vicious, starving guard dogs dotted around the city; it was a cheaper option for the banks than paying a security firm with static guards.

As was typical in most modern developments, neighbour's avoided conversation and eye contact, but Sophie had made the acquaintance of an elderly, trustful and talkative neighbor, a typical South Dublin trade down, widowed, in a house too big and expensive for her grown up children to maintain, or pay property tax on. They had sold it from under her, fudged the figures to their own benefit, and shoved her in a lonely one bedroom apartment. She lived alone, rarely visited, surrounded by remnants of furniture from her comfortable previous existence. No doubt the profits from the sale had helped offset some of her children's Celtic tiger acquired debt, which were the usual greedy bullshit; investment properties and holiday homes that were now strangling their cash flow. It was only a matter of time before they liquidated her last assets and shoved her in a nursing home to while away her last years.

Sophie had kindly offered to walk the old woman's dog, some breed of small yappy poodle, and had fed it some meat. Unfortunately it appeared that the dog had eaten something poisonous, it was a pity for Sophie, not because she was fond of the nocturnal barking dog, but it gave her great pleasure to see the little bastard licking his owners face following a walk and feed, she had also fucked up the poison dose and this pissed her off. Killing the yappy bastard had not been her intention.

CHAPTER 6

Sophie traced the edges of her boss's desk with her index finger before slipping behind it and settling into the comfortable studded leather office chair. It was far more comfortable than the generic office furniture she had in her adjoining office and this irked her.

She was about to go through the drawers when the desk phone rang, startling her, a quick glance at her watch told Sophie it was eleven A.M. and had to be the wife if her suspicions were correct, she felt a little thrill of butterflies and a sharp jolt of adrenaline pinch her guts, this was the beginning of the chase.

Normally when this call came her boss would retreat into his office closing the door behind him.

"Mr. O'Reilly's office, may I help you?" were Sophie's first words down the phone to her prey. There was a pause on the line before she heard Greta. "Oh, oh, is Mr. O'Reilly not there?" aha — Sophie detected a slight slurring of the words; this was good news, a morning drinker, a little glass of chardonnay to make the morning bearable. With utter politeness Sophie explained that no, Mr. O'Reilly was on a business golf day out, she didn't even ask who she was speaking to, she knew, Sophie explained that she had been trying to contact him herself without joy and that some important documents had come across her desk requiring Mr.O'Reilly's signature before business tomorrow, Sophie asked could she drop them off at his "residence" to be signed by him later. Greta hesitated then begrudgingly agreed to wait in while Sophie dropped them over as long as "she didn't take all day about it". By this very attitude Sophie knew that Greta was a pampered housewife, grown selfish, lazy and complacent at home, while her husband dealt with all the important stuff. Sophie had a feeling that perhaps Greta had a pressing engagement with a liquid lunch and an afternoon nap and didn't want anyone messing up her important plans.

Sophie swung her car out of the office car park, scuffing the low front of her car on the ramp and out of her designated parking spot which was worth €20,000 at the height of the boom, ridiculous.

She felt like a teenager on a day-trip leaving the city, a giddiness had started in her stomach and her senses were heightened, she plodded from one set of traffic lights to the next, avoiding the suicidal urban cyclists, ignorant bus drivers and bully boy taxi's. Until the city finally loosened its grip and she found herself sailing through the leafy suburbs of south Dublin, through areas that were familiar as she had grown up not too far from her destination.

She put on the car radio to some boring current affairs morning show, two self proclaimed "experts" were discussing the economy, immigration and the unemployment statistics which were still climbing at a worrying rate. "fucking cattle" she spat at the radio, she held contempt for anyone who didn't make an effort to keep or get a job, she hated Irelands new population of immigrants and migrant workers, she would never tell anyone that of course, that wouldn't be PC. "Fucking spongers" she shouted at the stereo before pressing the CD button to make the irritating broadcast go away.

She rolled up to a red light on the dual carriageway, and instantly felt her sixth sense telling her she was being watched. She checked her side mirrors before looking over at the white van in the next lane. It was such a cliché, she was being eyed up and having kisses blown at her by some tradesman or other, paint spattered raggedy T-shirt, two days stubble and likely stinking of body odour. This winking asshole really believed he was impressing her, especially when she smiled to herself, and gunned it from the lights. She would take the complimentary attention because of the day that was in it, any other day she would have given him the finger. She left him stuffing his face with a grease oozing breakfast roll far behind her at the lights.

Her mobile rang and she glanced at the number on the screen, her sister Charlottes' number, she put her eyes up to heaven and threw the phone onto the passenger seat, letting it ring out and go to message minder.

A few turns off the dual carriageway and she was in the leafy wide avenues of Foxrock. Passing the gated homes of old money and nouveau riche alike, this was like the embassy belt with mock Tudor, Georgian and Victorian homes, each trying to outdo the other in grandeur. It was renowned to be the best and most expensive place to live in Dublin. It had lost some of its charm during the boom years, some of the older, sprawling homes had been converted into apartments and it seemed that every house that once had expansive gardens were dotted with new bungalows and mediocre builds, some squeezed into corners of gardens, it smacked of greed.

Within a few turns she was outside the boss's house. She pulled into the driveway between two newly constructed granite gate pillars, there was an obvious gap in the neatly trimmed privet hedge next to the left pillar and she wondered if perhaps Mrs. O'Reilly had caused that bit of damage. The garden was mature, with neat beds and borders running the length of the driveway to the surprisingly modest, almost non-descript '70's style square home. The last of the summer blooms did nothing to raise her evaluation of the place. She was disappointed; it was a classic case of fooling the outside world into thinking a mansion sat behind the hedge and gate pillars. She drove past the front porch to a square parking area to the side of the house. As she cut the engine and put on her glasses she remembered to button up her blouse a bit more than usual. Sophie grabbed the unimportant documents, hitting the button to lock her car, as she gingerly approached the front door. She tapped the polished brass knocker on the mock Georgian front door and stood back off the doorstep. Immediately two small dogs were barking and scratching the inside of the door, when it finally opened, two west highland terriers spilled over the step and started jumping at the end of her trousers like she was a long lost friend, their claws raked her skin even through the trousers, and they left smears of drool and fur on her hem and shoes. The temptation to kick them and give them some air time over the hedge was overwhelming but she controlled it. Her shoes were glistening with slimy dog drool and she was raging, they were good Italian shoes and expensive, she had stupidly left her cheap Penney's shoes in the office. Sophie bent down to pet the excitable dogs and one of them timed his jumping just wrong; his canine tooth caught her knuckle, ripping the soft flesh, which instantly started to bleed. She looked up to see a brash bottle blonde in tight jeans, scuffed cheap runners and fleece jumper staring at her; "no fucking way" thought Sophie, "rough as a bears arse" was her first impression. "Come in" came a shout from somewhere further into the house and behind this vision of scruffiness, so this was just a cleaner or housekeeper.

The cleaner grabbed both dogs by the collar and dragged them back into the house, closing the door with her foot and gesturing Sophie to follow in the direction of the disembodied voice. Down the old fashioned hallway past hunting prints and a reproduction grandfather clock was the kitchen, she could hear the cleaner in an adjoining room praising the dogs with "Dobre, Dobre" she had encountered enough Polish people to know that this meant "good, good". It appeared that the slovenly hired help got her kicks when the dogs attacked visitors, a real endorsement of her contempt for her employer and guests, "a woman after my own heart" she thought, revenge comes in many forms and maybe this was her little indulgence.

The woman was clearly either Polish or eastern European, and her being here was so typical of south Dublin. No self respecting housewife in a good area survived without Filipino or eastern European housekeepers, cleaners, or nannies. Recession or not, women like Greta would be loath to loosing the hired help.

And there she was, Mrs. O'Reilly —Greta. Red eyes, yesterday's makeup and hair sticking up at the back betraying a bad night's sleep, and a grubby dressing gown that had no chenille left on it thanks to multiple laundering and age.

Sophie apologised for interrupting her while she "was obviously getting ready to go out", Greta waved a hand to dismiss the apology but the blatant relief was evident in her face, she honestly thought she had fooled Sophie into thinking she was getting ready, and not the reality that she had just crawled out of her crumpled lonely bed that she'd had all to herself for the past two years.

The bottle blonde cleaner lingered in the background, disinterestedly dragging and bumping a Hoover behind her and regarding Sophie with downcast eyes, she held little interest for Sophie, she was another of those women who had forsaken their families to live in a cat box apartment or shared accommodation in search of the illusive Celtic tiger fortune in western Europe, she would be lucky to get €200 per week for her servitude to spoilt rich bitches like Greta. Each day she would have to tolerate criticism, horrible pets, obnoxious guests and rude children, not exactly living the dream but Sophie felt neither pity nor concern for this woman.

She was just another foreign immigrant, it was impossible to ignore them anymore, every petrol station, fast food restaurant and grocery store seemed to have more than their fair share of this cheap labour.

It drove Sophie insane when she stood in a queue and heard foreign voices; she wanted them all to leave. It wasn't that she hankered for the old nostalgic days of old Ireland where everyone was white and catholic, she just didn't like this new wave of eastern European immigrants or Africans either. In modern Ireland they were part of the landscape, and it wasn't acceptable or politically correct to criticise them, not unless you wanted to be labeled a racist or fascist. Acceptance was being shoved down the public's throat from every angle.

She shook off the sudden dislike she had for the Polish cleaner and remembered why she was here, time to focus.

The kitchen was fairly new, spacious and modern and in total contrast to the put-on illusion of twee antiquity in the hall and other parts of the house Sophie had spied on the way in. this was a show kitchen —The type that demanding housewives badger their husbands for then don't ever make a decent meal in. food was not lovingly prepared here, laughter was not shared at the modern glass table or marble topped breakfast counter. Sophie noticed the ashtray, a strong brand of cigarette still smutting on the edge, it was all she could smell, no food or freshly brewed coffee, and judging by the amount of butts in the Waterford crystal ashtray, the woman was a heavy smoker that even the housekeeper couldn't keep up with, the butts were recent and numerous. Then she spotted the little brown plastic vial with a white top, sitting on the sink drainer; her perfect eyesight gave her the name "xanax". Greta realized she had spotted them and picked them up.

Sophie sucked at her torn knuckle and tasted the metallic tang of her own blood; she wouldn't mention the injury as it might offend Greta, this she did not want.

Greta snatched up the vial and deftly plonked it in on top of assorted mugs in a cupboard, "I'm getting over an awful dose of the flu, and these antibiotics don't agree with me, I hate taking them" offered Greta by way of explanation.

Sophie would be able to offer her something much stronger if the need arose. So far this woman was relaxed with Sophie, probably because she was in her own territory and the fact that Sophie's disguise as a dowdy plain assistant to her husband was working. The last time this woman judged her husband's underling as vivacious

—the woman got her marching papers from the firm once Greta had clapped eyes on her at the Christmas work party, the woman had done no wrong, but had simply been sacrificed for the sake of Greta's insecurities.

This was Sophie's ultimate rapport building exercise; she gave compliments on the house, made another apology for disturbing her and then re-visited the subject of the "antibiotics".

Sophie mentioned that her parents were GP's, father retired, but her mum still practiced, she could call her mum and arrange a prescription for a more gentle antibiotic if she liked? She casually dropped her mother's name and waited for the signs of recognition. Greta declined the offer but offered Sophie a coffee and asked about her family, confirming she knew her mother from school. She omitted to mention she was still very much her patient.

Mundane exchanges, but it seemed this woman was so starved of company that she was letting her guard down for the sake of idle conversation. Sophie knew that women like Greta loved to talk and control the conversation and that's exactly what Sophie allowed her to do, without any prompting she rattled on and before long was confiding in Sophie that she didn't get out much, all her friends were busy with careers or grandchildren, Sophie sat quietly, occasionally prompting, and allowed this woman her forum, and before long she had talked herself into a flood of tears, Greta lit yet another cigarette and drew on it greedily to steady herself with snot running down her top lip. Sophie could not believe her luck. Greta was spilling her guts, her loneliness, unhappiness, not feeling appreciated . . . it was all coming out.

Sophie allowed her vent until the storm had passed. She had to make sure there was no turnaround from the vulnerable woman, she couldn't allow her come to her senses through embarrassment, it wouldn't take much for the woman to realise her indiscretion and put her defenses back up so it was necessary to disarm her. Sophie couldn't afford to lose the advantage this tear filled conversation had given her, so she sprang from the chair and hugged Greta like a long lost pal, telling her how brave and brilliant she was.

She released Greta but stood back resting her hand on her arm, not quite disengaging from her. She offered, no, insisted on meeting Greta for a cup of coffee or a walk, just to get out of the house. Sophie wouldn't hear of any protest from Greta and she kept the woman busy and distracted by swapping mobile numbers, Greta was caught up in the momentum of Sophie's charm, refusal would seem ignorant and rude, Sophie's manipulation was passively working, Greta's face was crumpling up again and fresh snot was threatening to stream from her nose. "Time to get the fuck out of dodge" thought Sophie, so she hugged Greta again and made for the front door. As she drove past the porch there was Greta, weepy but waving and holding an imaginary phone to her ear and mouthing "I'll call you".

She drove back to the office floating, now she had to wait for the call from Greta she felt confident would come. She was so pleased at her progress that she felt a reward was in order. The only thing irritating her was the iridescent smear of snot on her shoulder from the blubbering woman.

CHAPTER 7

Her reward was to go fishing. Not the type of fishing done with rod and reel. Her version involved the internet. She had a variety of internet cafes she could use, all a decent distance from her apartment, she had handpicked them deliberately as they had no CCTV, just to be on the safe side she always wore a dark wig, baseball cap and clothes she only ever wore to these places, thank you "Dexter" for that tip.

She was aware that some companies used sneaky security measures to spy on staff; she definitely didn't want to get caught on camera because some idiot shop assistant was checking out porn while on the clock. She always used a different terminal and never went to the same café more than twice. She was acutely aware of spy cameras on staff —she had contacts in that business, she took no chances.

The wonderful world of Google gave her ample choice when it came to dating websites for Dublin singles. She had a membership with five sites at the moment, thanks to a postal order for €30 each month; they even provided her with a personalised e mail address, how kind.

"let's see who's fucking desperate" she thought as she turned the screen towards her, she sipped her latte while checking the latest profile matches, the list was endless, she had used a good looking girls image copied and pasted from the internet, there were similarities in looks, but it would never pass muster if used as a photo fit for her.

The sheer volume of desperate, horny, no strings attached guys out there in Dublin alone was staggering. It seemed that half the male population was suffering from permanent hard on. "Sad bastards" she thought flicking through the different responses to her profile.

She had a number of profiles set up depending on which site she was fishing on, she was a single executive, a hill walker, a girl getting over a break up; smacking of desperation, all the stereotypical profiles had worked so well for her. She looked at the responses and they fit the profile too —spoofers, the marrieds, baggage attached, separated and bitter, sad and lonely, she always looked twice at those; they were the easiest to lure for a date.

The sad and lonely types always thought their ship had come in; still, there was always the risk that they would brag before meeting up, simply because they couldn't believe their luck. She tried to avoid giving them the opportunity to shout from the rooftops and generally arranged to meet the night first contact was made. Giving a guy the chance and time to brag was risky.

Tonight she wanted to play it safe and pick a "discreet one night stand" sort of guy. Chances were they were in a relationship or married and wouldn't be shouting about a clandestine meeting via the internet. Guys like this were easy to make disappear by their very sneaky nature, the chances were nobody knew their plans or where they were going, and it was doubtful that she would be their first encounter.

She was like a barracuda when choosing her prey; with a couple of taps of her manicured nails she had e-mailed "ladiesman75".

His chosen name was in complete contrast to his profile, generic, screaming of desperation, and in his blurb he had written the line that had sealed the deal for Sophie – "been hurt before, broken engagement, now working in Dublin, no mates up here yet, would like to meet a kind lady with a GSOH who likes long walks, GAA and traditional music for no strings relationship". "Jesus fucking Christ" thought Sophie, this is one serious spoofer looking for a vulnerable woman or a complete looser with aspirations of being a ladies' man, out playing the field —this one would be interesting.

His profile was an anomaly, a change from the shifty married fifty year olds she could easily pick up at the driving range or the buff twenty something's from the gym, she could even pick up a date from the sad, broken hearted and lonely morons she met while walking the beach or the Dublin and Wicklow mountains. Scrap the discrete one night stand guys, this one will do.

She typed: "Johnny foxes pub by the fireside tonight, my real name is Ciara" and that was all it took to catch her fish.

The guys' profile photo reminded her of her childhood sweetheart Martin, an unassuming, shy guy with red hair, spurned by the other girls in her school clique. He made no demands on her through secondary school but when she entered college he became superfluous to her needs, and a drain on her free time once she discovered other activities. She'd dumped him in first year. She had broken his heart but he had no lasting effect on her, it was the first time in years he'd even crossed her mind.

"Johnny Foxes" pub was packed, it was high in the Dublin mountains and with its remote location it should be just another dying rural pub, the difference was that this pub catered for the tourist trade, it was packed to the rustic rafters with Irish brick a brack, the type most modern families had thrown out years ago, old pictures, posters and tin plate signs dotted the scarified shabby chic walls.

A roaring open fire and traditional music made it the perfect watering hole for any tourist searching for the Ireland that didn't exist anymore, — despite the brochures from Tourism Ireland. That canny government department would have any unsuspecting tourist believe that we still went around on donkey and cart with kreels of turf strapped to our raggedy friendly backs.

It was the ideal location for a date with a country bumpkin, his rural roots, love of traditional music and Gaelic football making the meet up point an easy choice, no city centre cocktail bar for this guy. The other factor that made the place ideal was the traffic of strangers through the door each night, they wouldn't attract attention.

The heat in the pub was stifling, rain soaked jackets steamed by the door and the music was already loud, the pub was doing a roaring trade in food and its smell mingled with the turf fire and smelly wet gear, it was nauseating to Sophie. A bus load of tourists stood around in groups laughing and slugging pints of Guinness, the fireside seats were taken up by a bewildered looking Japanese couple sipping glasses of the black stuff; it was clear by their winches that they hated it, but then no trip to Ireland was complete without trying it.

Sophie had chosen plain clothes and make-up to help her blend in, she looked like every other tourist that crossed the door here, the fireside seat was still being commandeered by the Japanese couple but she hung around anyway.

She wondered if anyone would make eye contact or approach her, if country bumpkin didn't show there were plenty of candidates here, the bumpkin was already fifteen minutes late and she was seething, and boiling in the scratchy woolen jumper.

Sophie had noted the lack of CCTV here; it was only over the tills. "Never mind the punters, watch the staff" she mused to herself, though, to be fair if she owned this place she'd do the same. The ringing of the tills almost kept pace with the "diddley eye" brand of Irish traditional music they were pumping into the bar.

To pass the time she graded every guy in the place, and guessed their occupation, nationality and level of difficulty in subduing.

Her choice of attire for the evening helped her blend it completely, hiking boots, water proofs and a wooly hat, she was burning with rage that he was late and worse that she was having to stand.

The Japanese couple must have been perceptive to her mood as the husband offered up his seat at the fireside, which she gratefully accepted and then turned her back to them to avoid being drawn into conversation; she had an ideal vantage point to watch the door.

Barreling through the door came a very flustered, red faced and soaking wet chubby guy with shocking red hair. This was her date, she recognized him instantly from his unflattering profile photo. He had obviously had to run some distance in the rain and his breath was ragged and his chest was heaving from the exertion.

They locked eyes as she waved him over, game on.

Poor bumpkin apologised profusely and nervously in a thick Cork accent, the "fecking taxi man" had left him further down the road than he thought and he'd run in the rain, that must have been a funny sight and it was a classic trick played by local taxi men on wet nights.

The bumpkin had some brass neck calling himself "Ladiesman" on his profile, he was nothing if not plain ugly, plainly dressed, supermarket branded jeans, cheap shoes and worse —bright carrot red hair, plain in every respect barring the red hair.

It didn't take Sophie long to asses this guy, he was a mummy's boy, careful with the pennies, working in the big smoke, from the grin on his face he couldn't believe his luck with the date, and this guy was not going home to his shared flat.

He was easily drawn into conversation, eager to impress her and becoming comfortable in the manipulated conversation. Too easily he gave up the information Sophie needed —he wouldn't be missed and hadn't told anyone where he was going.

This was going to be his one and only blind date.

It only took about an hour before the crowd started to press in on them and the music became louder, it was time to make her move now he was comfortable with her. She suggested they get out of her and go for a spin in her car to chat further.

He was out of his seat and helping her into her waterproof hiking jacket like a greyhound out of a trap, too eager.

Sophie ignored his pathetic wolf whistle and compliments on her car and slipped behind the wheel. Fast driving would not impress this guy and would increase his adrenaline levels, she did not want that, she kept a sedate, over cautious pace and nodded and agreed with every mundane comment he made.

Sophie really just wanted to accelerate and slam the brakes on to see his forehead smash off the dashboard, she had disabled the airbags for this purpose just in case that maneuver was ever needed, even the seat belt wouldn't save him as it was cut through and only held in place by bare threads.

She knew the back roads of the Dublin Mountains like the back of her hand; she knew which roads led into forestry, where there were no yellow and black barriers.

She memorised the maintenance roads, not even known by the joy riders who frequently came up here to drift stolen cars, do doughnuts, and then leave them burning and belching black smoke once they'd had their fun.

"Ladiesman" hadn't even realized just how far into the forest they had driven, he was far too busy regaling her with tales of rural Gaelic football matches with rival villages and the "almost" victories. She swung the car into a clearing, stopped and turned off her headlights plunging the car into darkness bar the dash display.

He looked startled and nervous; he had the fearful look of a teenager being propositioned on her Debs night. Sophie couldn't remember his first name but it didn't matter anyway, she turned to him seductively and asked if he was going to kiss her. "Ladiesman75" pounced like a leopard with wide eyes, his sharp teeth grated her lip which pissed her off, but she let it pass and returned his kiss like a pro.

He drooled and slobbered on her, forcing his tongue into her mouth and squeezed her thigh which she didn't mind, she knew once his dick was engaged his brain wouldn't be.

He never noticed her right arm reaching above to the sun visor, gently slipping out a primed syringe. She had already reached behind her and ever so slightly, opened her door, he hadn't noticed because she had disabled the internal lights on her car that should have alerted him.

She raised the syringe and plunged it into the side of his neck and leapt backwards from him, springing like a gazelle from the car. It was always better to beat a hasty retreat at these moments rather than risk being punched.

By the time she walked around to the passenger door the syringe full of vets sedative was kicking in, she yanked open the door and scolded him "ah ah ah, you won't be needing that, lover boy", she grinned at him as he gave up the mobile clutched in his hand, he hadn't even managed to unlock the keypad, never mind make a call before his world went dark, within seconds his phone was dismantled, with SIM card and battery safely thrown into the tree line. It didn't matter if the Gardai got a ping from here, the phones last location, they wouldn't find him. Just a broken up phone and a suspicion that this unhappy guy wanted to vanish. She was pleased, this was a new veterinary anesthetic she had gotten from Justin, and had been taking a chance using it tonight.

She coolly leaned in to recline his electric seat, he now just looked like a passed out boyfriend if anyone looked in, and they wouldn't though because he hadn't noticed her professionally tinted windows.

Almost everyone has heard the urban legend, the one where the guy wakes up in an ice filled bath minus a kidney, well for "Ladiesman75" it was becoming very real.

Thanks to a quick rifle through his wallet she now knew that "ladiesman75" was Gavin. He lay wallowing in the icy bathwater, gagged, cable ties cutting deeply into the flesh of his pudgy wrists and ankles, his pot belly floating above the ice cubes, skin a florid pink from the cold. He was still groggy but beginning to blink which meant the sedative was wearing off.

It was nothing but sheer bad luck that Gavin had ended up in a Jacuzzi bath in a penthouse apartment in Ballsbridge under the watchful eye of a psychopathic, uncaring and naked blonde who was shouting and roaring at him for being a "fat, heavy fucker"

She knew that the meeting in Johnny Foxes was a one off, she couldn't risk coming under suspicion. An American tourist had gone missing from that same pub almost a decade before, she had never been found and Sophie had heard all the rumors as to who had taken her, and all the feverish media speculation as to where she was buried. The most persistent rumour being, that she was in her final resting place under the golf course, just across the road, which had been under construction at the time of her disappearance. Her family regularly advertised for information and her name was well known to most Irish people, but still the silence continued for them.

Sophie knew better, Justin had confided in her one night while a bit stoned, that a local, small time crook and middle aged car dealer had drunkenly boasted to him that he was responsible for her disappearance, he had offered her a lift home, but things had gotten out of hand when she rebuffed his amorous advances, even when pressed by someone as persuasive and equally corrupt as Justin, he wouldn't give any more details, instead slugging down his pint he had roared "I didn't tell the guards, sure as fuck I'm not telling you" with that, he had slammed his pint glass on the bar and drunkenly lumbered out the door, full of drink, guilt and regret. It was the last he had spoken of it, to anyone.

There had been a number of women abducted over recent years but the Public and Gardai had decided who the prime suspect was. The public and media were always on the lookout for him, Facebook and twitter kept the public constantly on their guard and nervous if he was spotted. But Sophie knew he wasn't responsible for that one.

CHAPTER 8

Serial killers when interviewed, often complain that the most difficult part of the kill was not the act of taking of life, but the disposal afterwards. She had studied so many criminology, forensic and mass produced tomes on serial killers, most recently anything that could give her the edge on modern day forensics, she had expanded her book collection to entomology, psychology, chemistry and kept her mothers' well thumbed copy of Grey's anatomy for reference.

Shows like CSI had given the public false hope in modern forensics, in reality the tests required to give any clues were expensive and punitive on any police budget, and no, the results didn't pop up on the screen while they sat sipping lattes. The illusion of an ultra modern lab, complete with uber intelligent models, all of them clip clopping around in designer high heels was simply that, an illusion.

She had weighed up all the disposal options available to her. She had laboriously studied the tides in Dublin bay and decided that the chances were; body parts dumped in the polluted bay would wash up in a frothy scum, bumping onto the wave lapped shingles in one of the urban inlets or the east coasts' many beaches, rather than decompose on a long watery voyage in the Irish Sea. Dog walkers were notorious beach combers too, so that didn't help.

The tides and currents were notoriously fickle; anyway, she didn't own a boat, nor did she intend to.

Childhood memories of mackerel fishing with her family in a hired boat from Bullock harbor haunted her still, the irrational fear climbing down the quayside on a creaking slimy rope ladder, ever closer to the scuttling crabs in the shallow harbor water below. Being lifted by a rough, callous handed fisherman into a fragile, lobster tainted wooden row boat, complete with a puttering outboard motor. She shuddered at the memory, leaning over the side, seaweed and winkles dotting the encrusted paint sparse shiplap, her mothers' vice like grip on her waistband, sick as a dog, salty spray splashes stung her eyes and giant translucent jellyfish taunted her, bobbing in the passing swell, daring her to jump in to the green abyss. she hated that unsafe feeling when the boat was moving, swells thumping the bow, side sweeping currents lifting the whining outboard until the trough allowed it to bite in again and move forward. Fond memories flooded in though, of anchoring in the sheltered waters off Dalkey Island, this was the only time her sea sickness passed. Her sister was content to torment her and hum the famous music to "Jaws" even though she was scaring herself doing it.

Her father gingerly unraveling the lines and weights, and the final prize of being given the wooden handle, watching the line slice the water at an awkward angle, disappearing into the green depths, and not waiting long until a pull let you know a fish had eagerly impaled itself on the myriad hooks, another tug on the line, and another until the handle was trembling and vibrating in her grip, her terrified juvenile brain conjuring images of sharks or Dun Laoghaire's infamous giant conger eel on the end of the line. She recalled her father, legs braced like a prizefighter for balance against the sides of the rocking boat, reeling in the taught, spraying line, wet shimmering line, pooling in the bottom of the little row boat before finally hauling up a chandelier of flapping metallic fish. The sea breeze carried her mother's frenzied clapping with pride at the spectacle, waving to people watching from the Dalkey Island Hotel and her sister feigning aloof indifference peering above her copy of some teenage magazine.

She could remember the struggling, unhooked fish, battering themselves in defiance against the bottom of the boat, the cold feel of them with their spiky, slimy scales as she gripped each tail, following her fathers' lead, and bashing them against the "Y" shaped oar locks, silent now, eyes glossy and staring at the alien sky, sheets of newspaper draped across the spare seat board, sharp knife at the ready, copying her fathers' surgical knife strokes. Gangs of noisy sea gulls, scrabbling in mid air, waiting for the feast of guts at each throw of her fathers' strong arms. Her mother laughing, with the warm breeze catching her long blonde hair, and billowing it like a golden bridal veil behind her narrow shoulders, sun dappled, happy faces, and the joy of pouring sweet tea from a red tartan flask, adding the milk from a "Chivers" jam jar, the danger of leaning overboard to wash the sticky scales from their hands in the swell, silver specks tumbling down into the bottomless depths below like shiny pennies or glitter into a wishing well. Her father carefully tidying away the lines into the plastic shopping bag, snaring the lethal hooks into the spool of line till the next trip. They feasted like kings on a well earned egg sandwich, a packet of "Tayto" cheese and onion crisps, all downed with a cooling gulp of TK red lemonade. Her memories were anchoring snapshots of happiness.

Once the fish were wrapped in newspaper and put in the cool box for home, her sea sickness would return, and so would her misery at being on the bobbing swell.

She had ruled out using the Bay to dispose of waste and knew that flushing bits of a body down the Dublin sewer system were equally hazardous, so if you wanted to get caught courtesy of the Council or a company clearing a blockage you deserved to be locked up, for nothing if sheer stupidity.

Acid would ruin your bath, and who keeps industrial quantities in an apartment without attracting attention? Reciprocating power saws at three in the morning were bound to piss off the neighbours. There was no perfect formula, but Sophie had found a way that worked for her. She had read enough true crime books to avoid the obvious pitfalls. She drained the bodily fluids in the bath and dealt with the troublesome soft internal organs first, the stuff that will stink up your house and give the game away. This is where her dependence on the local dog population came in, at one stage she had considered running a dog walking service but had held back knowing that she would be glutinous in her killing sprees and maybe run the risk of becoming complaisant and sloppy. No, the only way was to reduce the body in stages; she had bought a very expensive mincer in a bespoke kitchen shop just off the capitals Grafton Street for this purpose, the rest was sheer graft, exhausting hard work and numerous varied trips.

The Dublin and Wicklow mountains, Sally gap, Kilakee forest provided the perfect dumping ground for anonymous looking lumps of flesh, the forests of the Dublin mountains had been used for years as the dumping ground for dogs, horses and other animals deemed unworthy of a backyard burial or veterinary attention.

On one occasion she could remember finding a recent looking human rib cage jutting out of the undergrowth in picturesque Kilakee woods; it shocked her and made her nervous, it was not one of hers. She had stood for twenty minutes under the crisp starlight with the sprawling lights of Dublin below, visible through the scraggly trees, her breath clouding up the air around her. She realized she was not the only one using this area, and then the visceral panic set in as she weighed up if she had been observed, the panic faded, and she chose a different location in future. Capable though she was, she did not want to tangle with a murderous male; her strength would only get her so far in a struggle.

For the larger body parts she also favored the moors for its remote drainage ditches and bog holes. The countryside was dotted with derelict, decrepit farms and seemingly bottomless lakes that studded the east coast of Ireland, it was on her doorstep and she took full advantage of it.

Sophie had become expert at reducing a full grown man or woman into seven or eight manageable bundles which could rest snuggly in identical hikers' backpacks, she looked no different to any other hill walker only that she chose the lesser known, more far flung and difficult routes through the mountains or forestry, the other hill walkers wouldn't notice that she was returning to her car boot for a fresh backpack every hour or so.

She recalled with a smile the last time she had brought her neighbours dog with her. She'd sat and had sandwiches, savoring a flask of coffee on a rocky outcrop, smoking while day dreamily overlooking the tangled valley in the Dublin Mountains. Mean while the dog feasted greedily on the meat she provided from a soggy sandwich bag, she had sat transfixed while the dog had rolled and snuffled along the ground a large pink kidney as if it was a ball, before wolfing it down in one go.

She had wondered for ages if there were others like her operating in Ireland and the ribcage in Kilakee woods had confirmed it for her. It had been recently announced that Dublin was to receive an incinerator to dispose of household waste, this made her smile, landfill was far too risky but this new piece of infrastructure might make her life easier in future.

It was well known that Ireland had a serial killer operating in the East coast but so far only women had disappeared. When men vanished it was generally accepted that it was due to drug debt or the spiraling gangland crime problem, some even put it down to depression or running away from their debts, understandable, given how aggressive the banks were recently. Sadly, some had even felt so powerless in the grip of debt, that vanishing, only to be found a few days later, hanging from a tree, was their only escape from the relentless pressure. The male suicide rate was a sad indictment of the countries desperate situation, and the vile treatment being meted out by the banks and their minions.

Of all the crime literature she had read it seemed that profilers favoured gender on gender killers, how wrong she thought. Amazing that the FBI could be so cocky and short sighted. She didn't have any preference.

Something had bugged her for a while, she had watched a channel 4 documentary on serial killers and it had left her with more questions than answers. "Psychopath night" had ignited some serious soul searching in her.

She didn't fit the so called "psychopath spectrum". This was the accepted and definitive list of personality traits attributed to serial killers; she ran through them in her mind, anylising the nuggets of wisdom by various academics featured on the program.

As children psychopaths and serial killers were supposed to be cold and callous, uncaring to anyone, even their parents. That didn't make sense to her. She got on well with her childhood friends and her parents. She could recall an incident in secondary school of standing up to a bully, that didn't make her callous, surely? She was protecting the underdog!

A timid, inoffensive girl had been unmercifully bullied and was eventually pushed down the stairs by a nasty girl. A girl imbedded in the schools "IT" crowd, the cool, nasty, mean girl brigade endemic in most Irish schools. When the bullied girl returned to school a few weeks later on crutches and sporting a cast on her broken leg; the bully made a bee line for her, immediately resuming her taunting. Sophie and her friends had watched in horror as the bully pushed and made fun of the injured girl, goading her. Without a second though Sophie had walked up to the bully and punched her straight in the face, breaking her nose and causing the bully to spray the convent walls and holy pictures with bright red blood. How did that make her callous? She asked herself. It had earned her a three week suspension and the admiration of her parents and peers.

Years later she had learned that the bully was a messed up junkie, shoplifting and turning tricks for her next hit, "that's karma, bitch" she thought.

Like bullet points firing in her mind she went through each label on the spectrum and could disassociate herself from most of them. She had never set fires, never been cruel to animals; in fact she preferred animals to humans.

Envy, no, she couldn't agree with that, she was never envious of the attention her sister got. If anything, she had orchestrated it to deflect attention from herself, and anything she truly wanted she worked hard to get. She never felt envious of her friends with their nice boyfriends and attentive husbands. She had never experienced envious maternal brooding watching them bounce their babies on their laps. This envy label made no sense to her.

Boasting? Sophie could never lay claim to that little sin. She had observed her school friends boasting about various triumphs real or perceived and could tell immediately when they were lying. There was no way was she going to be caught out under scrutiny. She kept her triumphs under wraps.

The only time she felt the "superiority complex" label was when she had someone prone, either in bed, her bath or unconscious in her car. So yeah, she could give them that one, but then who doesn't occasionally feel superior at a job well done?

"Intolerance to criticism"; that was a strange one. Most people she knew were intolerant, it was human nature to defend yourself when under attack, it just depended how much of a scene you made. Any criticism directed at her had been few and far between; she had sucked it up, looked contrite, accepted it gracefully and moved on, even though she literally, wanted to murder the person.

There were some traits mentioned on the spectrum she could relate to but then so could most of the population at one stage or another. Going by the description she could picture the people around her that were successful, happy, driven and got the job done. The list seemed vague and generic to her, bullet points cherry picking the faces people sometimes showed and sometimes concealed.

As a final act of defiance she printed off the list and ran her index finger down each point, pausing occasionally to confirm or refute whether it reflected her personality.

"Betrayal", "Egocentric", "Grandiosity", "Hubris", "Shamelessness", "superficial charm", "superiority complex", "tantrums", "vanity", "manipulative", "perfectionism". Jesus, they were talking about most of the women she knew. If anything it described her sister to a "T".

It was bullshit. If that's all they had to go on it would be a while before any profiler came up with a decent description of her.

It was final then. She wasn't a psychopath, just a girl who got her kicks from snagging a guy and taking out her frustrations on him.

CHAPTER 9

Her boss never mentioned her unnecessary trip out to the house, most likely in the hope that she hadn't noticed, or had chosen to turn a blind eye to the dysfunctional world that was his family home, it could have been sheer embarrassment that kept him from mentioning it, either which way, Sophie didn't give a shit.

The first phone call from Greta came on a wet Wednesday afternoon, she was tentatively looking to meet up for a cup of coffee, this was not helpful, a walk would offer distractions to talk about, a confined coffee shop would prove a bad location if there was a lull in the conversation, it could cut this embryonic friendship dead if Greta felt uncomfortable at all.

She suggested meeting her somewhere else, a somewhere she could get a few "looseners" into her, and suggested a well known and respectable pub in up-market Leopardstown that was only a short drive from Greta's home.

The pub was quiet enough as it was early evening, due to the pinch of the recession most people were loath to be seen as frivolous with their disposable income, and the only patrons seemed to be the usual respectable bar flies and a group of middle aged golfers creating their own background chatter.

The golfers occasionally punctuated the murmur with raucous laughter and schoolboy back slapping. Sophie didn't trust the golfers, never picked one as her target as she was always amazed how emotionally stunted men felt it ok to open up while completing 18 holes, sensitive conversations would be had on a par 3 that otherwise, in any other setting, would never take place. Dangerous and best avoided.

She had chosen a discrete window seat overlooking the pubs car park. She was out of the direct line of sight of the golfers, and veiled by a large well tended ficus plant. She spotted Greta pulling into the ample car park, watched her gingerly try to reverse the car into a spot, make a mess of it, drive out and pick a different one.

Her nervousness and crap parking was a telling sign, Sophie's job was to put this woman completely at ease from the minute she walked in if she was to get anywhere with this plan. Two glasses sat in front of her, dripping with condensation, one, a double gin and tonic, the other – just tonic water. No prizes for guessing who the double was for.

Greta pushed open the double doors and nervously looked from left to right, hesitating, as she did so the door swung closed behind her, trapping her oversized and expensive handbag. Sophie noticed the wide eyed look of panic and immediately left the booth as Greta blushed under the gaze of the now silent observers from the golfing party, like a gazelle Sophie sprang into action and freed the bag, leading Greta away from the doors.

Her presence offered courage and solace to the self conscious and embarrassed Greta. Sophie quickly turned her back to the golfers just in case any of them decided to try the chat up lines that came easy after a successful round of golf and some pints, the element of male bravado always came to the fore when they were in groups, and they became predators, like the gangs of schoolboys hanging around the bus stop harassing girls.

At the seats she noticed Greta looking at the two glasses with trepidation, so while still standing, Sophie picked hers up, took a big slug and said "I think we deserve this after making it past that pack of hyenas" and sat down. She gave Greta a smirk, playing the female comrade card and pushed the gin and tonic towards Greta, any chance she had to refuse the drink had passed and refusal would look childish and rude.

The conversation eased in gently and a few drinks later Greta was again given the stage to waffle about her dogs, her rubbish housekeeper —who was stealing from her by the way, — she just couldn't prove it. She spoke about her sons, glowing with maternal pride, both doing brilliantly in college but far too busy to visit their mother, invisibly steering the conversation Sophie led her to talk, compliant Greta became more relaxed and talkative, and didn't notice how often her drinks were being replenished by the lounge girl at Sophie's expense.

Sophie had already spoken to the barman before Greta's arrival, and had told him in a secretive and hushed tone that she was only three weeks pregnant, —a total lie. She hadn't told anyone yet, and that if two gin and tonics were ordered hers MUST be just tonic water. The barman had delighted in this secret, and had called the lounge girl over and given strict instructions in accordance with Sophie's plan.

Greta became more animated, more drunk, and the walls to her personal life tumbled down with every inebriated word, while Sophie had the full advantage of being sober as a judge.

The level of contempt this woman felt for everyone around her was astounding. In her prime she had been an airhostess with Aer Lingus, back in the days when it was a glamorous and elite profession. Only open, according to Greta, to women with looks, class, impeccable manners and background, she bitched for twenty minutes about the standard of today's air hostesses, it was draining to listen to, but Sophie knew this was a task no different than any other she had to endure. Though, if she made one more reference to today's airhostesses looking like hookers, she may be tempted to smash her face off the gin splashed tabletop, right there and then.

It was amazing how much she opened up to Sophie, a complete stranger —it was like free therapy, cathartic, and she was getting a visible high by off loading. She railed on about her lonely, purposeless life, empty nest syndrome, and her "bloody" husband not worth making an effort for anymore and who had no interest in her anyway as she grew older.

It was Sophie who called a halt to the meeting, not wanting Greta to be too pissed to drive home, and citing work as her reason to call it a night. She walked the unsteady Greta to her car, intently listening to the garbled, giddy ranting of the very tipsy woman, she watched as the chubby drunkard flopped behind the wheel and started the car, over-turning the key and nearly burning out the ignition coil.

The idiot almost demolished a bollard on the way out as she was too fixated on waving to Sophie, the only damage being a nice fresh scratch down the passenger side of her already drink damaged car.

The cold leather seats were a comfort after the meanly padded bench seat in the pub, she put her head back, and closed her eyes for a few seconds just to clear her thoughts and get that stupid woman's voice out of her ears. She mentally assessed whether the meeting had gone well. Turned the key illuminating the dash, and instantly felt a flicker of anger that she had spent so much time with that inane woman. She stabbed the CD button with her finger, flicked on the headlights and gunned it back to the motorway. The lingering stench of Greta's perfume from the parting bear hug pissed her off even more as she buzzed down her window, and lit a cigarette to mask the smell. Each encounter with the woman left its mark on her, whether it was snot, smeared make up on her shoulder, or pungent perfume. There was no getting away from the woman.

CHAPTER 10

The text messages began the next morning. It was like teenage banter, but reading between the lines Sophie knew this woman was delighted with her new pal.

"My head is pounding! Hope you're ok in work today, LOL!" "Fucks sake" whispered Sophie to herself. "Exclamation marks and LOL" —for fucks sake. Greta must have picked that up from one of her sons, thinking it was cool.

She went back to her monotonous paperwork, determined not to answer the text for at least an hour, just to give the impression that she actually gave a shit about her job. Let her wait. She imagined the gin sozzled and hung-over woman lolling around her sterile kitchen, chain smoking and waiting with giddy anticipation of a reply.

Sophie's plan was coming together, she was roping this woman in slowly, and not so difficult after all if you can spot a character flaw or weakness. A few more meetings like this and maybe pushing the boundaries; becoming more tactile would leave Greta defenseless when Sophie made her amorous move. She had to get Greta to a place and state of mind where she would be trustful, compliant, comfortable, and safe, so that any sexual advance would seem natural and even exciting and anticipated. She wanted Greta to the grateful for the advance when it came.

CHAPTER 11

Sophie monitored Facebook and "missing persons Ireland" websites regularly; it came up automatically on her Facebook newsfeed. She sipped her latte in an underused café around the corner from her office; they were still charging sky high prices for coffee, so it guaranteed a fleeting and permanently sparse clientele.

She stared blankly at the picture on the smart phone screen of her last kill. Quizzically she raised her eyebrows as she pondered whether his roommates had any idea what had happened to their lodger. He had walked off the face of the earth —literally. Sophie knew where he was, but heavy rain and early snow were not going to help anyone else locate him.

The fact that his post got so many "likes" and shares didn't even stir pity in her, then again, people would share and like anything, if only to be part of the collective, the pity parade. It made them feel like they were helping, Sophie found it fascinating, like those people who believe on Facebook that if you "click "like" to send a prayer to this sick child" it actually did any good, pathetic.

She updated her Facebook feed, and touched base with a couple of old school friends she kept in touch with, a little contact every now and then kept them happy.

She went back to her plain covered book —"Gates of Janus" by the notorious English "moors murderer" Ian Brady. This book was truly frightening and had been on the Irish banned book list for years, she had bought it online from a UK supplier a while back, and was fascinated by it, he spoke hypothetically in the book about the mind of a killer, never admitting to his own crimes but in a very persuasive way he was able to justify his actions, and anyone susceptible to suggestion would buy into his brainwashing style of writing, no wonder it was banned.

And yet it echoed her owns thoughts, doubts and reasoning. In this book she found a kindred intelligence, a justification for her actions that she couldn't find anywhere else.

She had considered writing to him in prison but knew that was a really bad idea unless you want to be "flagged" by the authorities, she had even considered writing a book and using it as an excuse to make contact with him and pick his brains. She longed to have a conversation with him but knew it was never to be.

There were so many serial killers she would love to have spoken to, Aileen Wournos –rough but interesting, and her favorite for nothing if sheer savagery —Ted Bundy. Unfortunately for her, both had been executed, so she would have to make do with imaginary conversations in her head.

She shook herself back to reality and work; a meeting had been scheduled for her for the afternoon, a new prospective client in one of Dublin's industrial heartlands. To the west of the capital lay a sprawl of bleak, half occupied industrial estates.

This bakery business had been set up during the recession and had obviously taken advantage of a vulnerable landlord to be able to afford the rent for three adjoining commercial units.

She knew from a friend in real estate how expensive the rent here had been during the boom, now landlords were willing to sell their souls to get a tenant and keep the aggressive banks off their backs.

This was not an area of Dublin she was fond of. It was working class, marginalized and tough. It bore the scars of generations of crime and neglect; it was rife with criminals and short on civic pride.

Public green spaces and derelict plots were dotted with raggedy half starved and neglected pie-bald horses, Tethered on rusted, tangled chains or makeshift frayed ropes to the muddy rutted ground. Some just stood there, resigned to their fate and lack of care, others endlessly plodded the length of their ropes, aching for the longer grass beyond and forever out of reach.

Sophie locked the car doors and gingerly made her way through the sprawl of council estates; it was an ill advised shortcut, she kept a close eye on her side mirrors at every red light, the area was notorious for carjacking.

Dilapidated buildings and boarded up council houses were interspersed with the occasional well kept home where hard work and pride still lived. Zombie like junkies shuffled along the paths in ones and twos and bored teenagers in tracksuits and hoody's hung around the street corners, their presence a menace enough to any passerby.

The residents had the same grey pallor as the buildings around them. Even the row of shops at its heart spoke of the area, Pub, bookies, chipper, off license; they were the only retail outlets needed in an area like this.

A harsh breeze laced with sleet blew down from the dark hooded mountains in the distance; it did nothing to wash away the grime and deprivation that clung to this tough area like a sickness.

Walls were tattooed and tagged with graffiti; at least they added a splash of colour to the broken grey edifices lining the road into the commercial estate. Their tagging bore legend to the frustration and anger of local youths. Disillusionment and hopelessness was etched on the broken abused buildings of the area.

She turned into the industrial estate through high imposing steel gates, the perimeter topped with razor wire, evidence of failed break-ins dotted the wire, and rags of torn tracksuit tops fluttered with discarded plastic bags at odd spots, rubbish and clothing alike impaled on the surgical sharp coils.

She pulled the car over outside a vacant building before getting to the unit, and sat quietly pulling on a cigarette until a couple caught her eye. She watched them get out of their well kept and mediocre saloon car, both were well dressed and about the same age as her parents. They just didn't look like they lived around here. They were gathering up discarded wooden pallets.

The husband stomped on the pallets to break them up, snapping the backs of the wooden platforms, while the wife loaded each scrap into the boot and across the back seat, both were nervous and looking around. It took a minute for Sophie to figure out what they were doing, and then it dawned on her; firewood. Another recession hit couple making a trip to unfamiliar territory, praying they wouldn't be recognised, and doing whatever it took to keep some heat in the house.

The hard times had affected most families, some more than others, parents were skipping meals just to make sure the kids had food or worse; the mortgage was paid to the now unfriendly and eviction frenzied banks.

The hardship wasn't helped by the punishing taxes brought in by the disappointing new government. Hard pushed families were resorting to approaching money lenders for cash for basic provisions; they were swapping one wolf at the door for another.

She had to applaud this couple for their ingenuity, better than sitting in the cold shouting at some inept politician on TV. The

Christmas music and ads seemed like a sarcastic soundtrack to watch this couple to. It was pitiable, and she could see the shame on their faces as they huddled close, whispering together, they realised she had been watching them.

She pitched her cigarette butt out the window; her litter wasn't going to make any difference to the area and saved them their blushes by nudging her car away, leaving them with their shame to gather up the splintered kindling lying on the road.

Her meeting had been arranged with a bakery owned by some Polish businessmen. They expressed a wish to promote themselves under the guise of "Irish owned/Irish jobs" knowing full well that people were feeling particularly patriotic at the moment, and not wanting to miss out on that unique selling point.

It took only twenty minutes and a tour of the sweetly scented bakery for her to realise that each and every employee down to the floor sweeper was eastern European. There wasn't a single Irish person in the place unless you counted the young Irish intern working for free answering their phones, cheap labour was now free labour, thanks to the Irish government and their "job bridge" scheme.

Professionalism was the name of the game today. It meant a healthy commission and an advertising campaign to keep her workdays busy. She could throw her opinions and ethics out the window when it came to business. These guys were arrogant, hardnosed businessmen who only thinly veiled their dislike for Irish people.

She should have left there with the sweet smell of freshly baked bread clinging to her suit and saliva pooling in her mouth; instead, she had an aching jaw from fake smiling and a nasty taste in her mouth only relieved by cigarettes, chain smoked in the traffic. Still, the signed and lucrative PR contract sat on her passenger seat, the shadows cast by sleet on the windscreen dappling the cover all the way back to the office.

CHAPTER 12

Sophie's sister Charlotte was your generic and sadly typical south Dublin "smug married". She had met Gerald or "Ger" as he preferred to be called at a charity ball in one of Dublin's swanky Celtic tiger hotels. Charlotte only attended the ball to see and be seen and the bitch gloried in the chance of rubbing shoulders and hobnobbing with some of Ireland's minor celebrities.

She didn't give a shit about the charity and paid for the ticket and nothing else, it was the bragging power it gave her, she was as shallow as they came, she worked as a librarian which gave her an air of academia even though she wasn't that smart. Still, the job gave her credibility and the work was a doddle if not repetitive and unchallenging. It also gave Charlotte plenty of time during the day to update her Facebook page with funny anecdotes, videos of cats and lots of time to sip tea reading the gossip magazines.

She was an older version of Sophie in the looks department, though her features were not as sculpted, she had fleshiness to her jowls since marriage, and her hair was a natural dirty blonde as opposed to Sophie's flaxen natural colour.

As children they had been almost identical but their physical appearance had meandered down different paths since puberty.

Ger was an accountant and investment banker for one of the larger Irish banks that could be considered the protagonist of the property bubble and Celtic tiger crash. His ego had allowed millions in property loans to be issued on his "say so" to developers. He was average height, typically unattractive and pale Irish man with a paunch and prematurely receding hairline. He liked to brag about his prowess on the rugby pitch as a young man, but Sophie could smell a lie from a thousand yards. He had attended a renowned South Dublin school where playing rugby and networking were more important than exam results, his school connections had got him on the career ladder to start with. Not that he'd ever admit that.

He had had to re-invent himself since the bust, and changed the colours of his flag to stay relevant to the bank. His reincarnation led to him now being the teeth of the bank, repossessing and calling in the loans that he had originally dispensed like sweets. He was now the head honcho of debt collection and by adapting, had assured himself a prolonged seat at the table of corporate gluttony. He made a good salary and commission liquidating and retrieving the debts for the bank from the poor bastards he gave the loans to in the first place.

Sophie hated him with a passion, still, she could see why her sister found his smug confidence attractive, they were two sides of the same coin, adaptable, self confident, smug, greedy and shallow. They were insanely loyal to each other which afforded them the best Dublin lifestyle.

The first day Charlotte and Ger moved into their overpriced executive home in the seaside idyll of Greystones, Sophie had called in with a housewarming gift, an expensive coffee machine from Dublin's best department store —Brown Thomas.

It seemed an appropriate gift for two "yuppies" moving into an old money area.

That was the day Ger made a near fatal mistake. The bastard had brushed his groin against Sophie's ass while she filled the kettle at the sink, there had been an unspoken hatred between them ever since. For her part, not out of loyalty to her sister, but sheer venomous disgust at his brass neck; and for his part — that she had not reciprocated his advance, and the faint possibility that she could at any time disclose his indiscretion.

It was another Sunday lunch at her mother's house and her mother had been chirping away for a few minutes before Sophie snapped back to reality, realising her mother had mentioned Greta, she went on alert, "what, sorry?" —"I said have you heard anymore about poor ole Greta?" her mother repeated. "Honestly Sophie, I don't know where your brain wanders off to half the time, bloody Walter Mitty sometimes". Sophie's brain was retracing the steps of her last two disposals and mentally check-listing her precautions.

Thankfully her mother's attention wandered as much as hers, moving on to some piece of trivial gossip being espoused by her sister. Charlotte sat swishing her dark blonde hair, and went on to gossip about some Irish model having an affair with some decrepit old developer worth squillions (her sisters words) Sophie knew this rumour to be true, as she'd seen them together but she wasn't going to give her sister the satisfaction of having confirmed gossip.

Sophie could attest to three members (married) of the Irish rugby squad who had offered their sexual services to her in one of Dublin's VIP nightclubs on different occasions, but she favoured discretion. If there was one thing she knew about the big fish in the little Irish celebrity world – they loved being talked about. They would sell their soul to be "papped" for the Sunday gossip columns. The last thing she wanted was to be photographed on the arm of some attention seeking fool.

And so, another painful Sunday lunch with the smug pair, bragging about how well Ger was doing retrieving the debts for the banks, like it was a public service.

He bragged about a builder he was dealing with, a celebrity chef with a failed restaurant and a couple of guys in the motor-trade. This last mention caught Sophie's ear as that was Justin's trade —her shag buddy and drug supplier. She dropped his name into the conversation and waited for Ger's ego to grab it.

"oh that one, yeah, he's stuck into the bank for a bit alright, but he's playing ball at the moment so I don't need to give him my attention, yet", Sophie looked over to see her Sister rubbing Ger's arm and glowing with pride, her silver streaks through her blonde hair sparkling under the harsh kitchen lights. Sophie glared at this show of affection and Ger caught the look. Through a mouthful of roast potatoes he quizzed her as to how she knew this bad boy with a dodgy reputation. He dropped the bomb and sat back in his chair with a smug "fuck you Sophie" expression on his face.

This meant only one thing, her mother was now going to quiz her as to how she knew this dodgy character, so Sophie quickly concocted a story that her friend was dating him. She was surprised he had legitimately borrowed money for the business; so many small time motor dealers in Dublin were funded by the proceeds of crime, namely drugs money. It was the perfect avenue to launder dirty money and the criminal assets bureau couldn't keep up.

She could feel her mother's gaze on her face and hoped she wasn't involuntarily blushing. Ger continued knowing he had centre stage, "Ah I've heard stuff about that fella; still, as long as he keeps paying me I don't give a shite about his other activities". now her mother was interested, but Sophie zoned out as both her mother and Ger sat gossiping about Justin and his shady dealing, Ger didn't know the half of it, but the tidbits of gossip he was feeding her rapt mother was enough to get Sophie very pissed off, she knew that if Justin was aware of this gossip and indiscretion Ger would get a visit from a few guys in a van some evening; whether he was a high up bank official or not.

Her comeback caused consternation at the table when Sophie innocently enquired of Ger as to "how his hair transplant was settling in and was it worth the money?" Her mother bolted out of her chair shouting her name, but Ger sat transfixed, loaded fork halfway to his mouth and her sister lunged like a cheetah across the table spitting like a cobra. "Couldn't help yourself, could you? Totes bitchy Sophie!" on hearing her stupid sister use that stupid colloquialism Sophie knew she had achieved victory by striking the right nerve and went for the jugular.

"They transplant tough ole pubic hair don't they? So that would make you —a dick head?"

Her father had been dumbstruck up to now but he spat a mouthful of food clear across the table and burst out laughing. With hoots and exclamations of "oh Jesus, Jesus!" and peels of belly laughs he stood up from the table and made for the sitting room and the rugby match, with a sheepish Ger following, like a kicked puppy at his heels.

Charlotte busied herself loading the dishwasher while her mother silently cleared the table, the only sign of annoyance was when the plates were unceremoniously dumped on the kitchen counter, "Out of order young lady" was all her mother said, though, she could see the edges of her mother's mouth trying not to smile.

They all knew Ger had been to one of those hair restoration clinics, it was cosmetic frivolity to keep up with the burgeoning female market. It was a procedure that had remained unmentioned up to now, even when Ger had arrived for Sunday lunch with a red scalp, raw visible puncture marks on his newly shrunken forehead. Sophie had been tempted to pass comment weeks ago but had been given "the look" by her mother that told her it was wise to let it go; now Ger's not so secret hair transplant was out in the open and a source of embarrassment and discomfort this Sunday. Still, Sophie drove home smiling that evening.

Ger was like a raw wound to Sophie, and any little victory was welcome, had Ger any idea what she could do to him, his manners would have been better. She had fantasized a number of times of having a meek, incapacitated Ger in her bathtub, that would be the time she didn't give a shit what noise the neighbours heard, still, her sister would be left alone and bitter if Ger ever disappeared, and that would mean one thing, she would be a pain in the ass and a drain on her parents, she wasn't about to let that happen.

Whether she liked it or not Ger would have to be tolerated. Still, she allowed herself to day dream; it just meant some other poor bastard would suffer the fate Ger deserved.

CHAPTER 13

She had fucked up royally, one of her backpacks had a tear in it which meant somewhere in the Wicklow mountains was a shred of material with DNA evidence on it, degraded by the weather or not it was a royal fuck up. She mentally retraced her steps, physically doing so was risky. Where the fuck could she have snagged it? She tried to brush it off, her brain debating whether she was panicking for nothing or did she have a real problem.

"FUCK! FUCK! FUCK!" she roared stomping around the apartment dragging the torn backpack behind her like a limp ragdoll. This was not good, she was normally so careful but this was a major oversight. If it was caught on a bush far from her dump site it was ok, but if it acted like a marker and drew someone's attention then it spelled trouble."BOLLOX" she roared at the ceiling.

The gym was the only place to burn off the rage at her own stupidity, but even the toughest, most punishing machines didn't help, her relief came from exhausting herself at the punch bag in the mainly male section. She was utterly unaware of the looks her male counterparts gave her as she beat the bag with the venom of a middleweight champion. No one dared approach her except a misguided trainer asking did she need help, when he was given a curt "fuck off" he returned to the female gym bunnies, tail between the legs and a little freaked out.

Sleep did not come easy that night, especially since the piece that had ripped formed part of the yellow buckle that tightened the shoulder straps and Sophie knew that a plastic buckle would make a brilliant contact material for transferred DNA and fingerprints —hers.

She mentally tortured herself all the next day, even breaking her cardinal rule of never revisiting a dump site, she took her expensive camera with telephoto lenses and curb crawled along the mountain road she suspected as the place the buckle had been lost, avoiding the pot holes and bracken rimmed ditches.

With the camera and lens stuck out through the car window she looked like a tourist, anxious for a good nature shot but unwilling to brave the elements outside the car.

After an hour of limping along surveying the tree-line, she gave up. The afternoon light was fading and grey cloud, heavy with hail and sleet was rapidly making its way across the mountaintop moor in her direction. The weather was notoriously fickle so high up and it was time to head home.

She wound down the narrow road cut from the edge of a steep cliff overlooking one of Wicklow's scenic lakes, if she looked over the edge of the low stone wall she could see the mansion owned by the renowned Guinness family. She had no interest in the sights today.

A small group of native red deer led by a regal buck suddenly belted across the tree lined road in front of her. The buck bore huge untrimmed antlers streaming velvet like Christmas garlands. They were trying to get to the tree line opposite, she slammed on her brakes to avoid hitting the young does that made up the straggling and nervous rearguard, a thought crossed her mind as she sat with the engine idling watching the group scatter across the weather beaten and scarred tarmac, "stupid females following the buck". The magnificent buck stood eyeing her defiantly, puffing clouds of breath in a halo, his bulk straddling the verge till the last nervous doe had crossed, and then ran, head held high to catch up with his herd.

It reminded her of a framed print in her parents rarely used "good room" of the "Monarch of the Glen".

CHAPTER 14

It was a miserable, damp winters' Saturday when she reluctantly dragged herself from her warm bed.

Within minutes the aroma of fresh coffee filled the chilly apartment. She sipped it slowly savoring the dark nutty brew. She lit a cigarette and drew heavily on it before stubbing it out in her pristine sink.

Her next task was to check the large rectangular Tupperware boxes she kept stacked under the sink, closest to the heat from the dishwasher beside it.

There were ten in all; each contained a piece of mouldy bread in varying degrees of decay. There was a particular type and colour of mould she was looking for – Aspergillus. A yellow or black spot mould. She discarded eight of the ten boxes full of green mouldy bread. Two contenders left, she lifted the boxes one by one up to the light in the kitchen, examining the contents from all angles through the murky Tupperware.

She left the boxes on the counter and crossed over to the chrome American fridge, taking out two wedges of cheap supermarket Brie cheese, she unwrapped them and carefully pierced each piece about ten times right through with florist wire, she put each slice of Brie in each of the Tupperware boxes and put them back under the sink, they would be ready in about three weeks for what she had in mind.

This was homemade blue cheese but it would be lethal. She took out a batch she had made weeks before and examined it under the light, it looked perfect, the Brie still held its shape but she could see where the mould had wormed its way into the piercings.

She ripped open the orange net holding the daffodil bulbs from the garden centre, put on a paper dust mask and rubber gloves and started peeling and chopping the bulbs, she put them to gently simmer in some butter in the pan till they were soft then added sugar and a cup of antifreeze and left the heat on low to reduce the liquid, this was not the type of onion marmalade or chutney you gave to guests you liked.

Her next job was to mix the fiberglass with the flour mixture to make up the dough for the crackers, she gently baked them in the oven and took them out to cool and crisp.

There was Christmas shopping to be done first before she could contemplate getting ready.

She was looking forward to this date, but this poor bastard was not going to enjoy the snacks she had made for him. His profile may have stated that he "likes fireside chats, good cheese and a crisp glass of wine". At least the wine would be cool and crisp with an undetectable hint of Rohypnol.

She had taken a few days leave from work just to watch the effect her "snacks" would have on this guy and she was excited.

She decided to head into town and treat herself to a new outfit, it had been a hard week. She parked her car in St. Stephens green and daydreamed all the way down the steep escalator to the bustling shops below.

The centre was busy with people doing early Christmas shopping, it seemed Halloween didn't count anymore; everyone was in a rush to get to the biggest celebration of the year, amazing how a recession can make people grab at moments of levity like a life buoy.

Sophie made a point of avoiding eye contact with shop assistants, she need not have worried, each clothes shop she entered had the same clones, wandering around, bored and disinterested in talking to customers. She picked a few items in her size, paid and left without a word being exchanged with any other human.

She decided to wander out of the shopping centre and stroll down Grafton Street and soak up some Christmas atmosphere. There might even be some bargains in the pre-Christmas sales; office party season was fast approaching which meant plenty of single lonely guys looking for love and company over Christmas.

She always noticed a spike in activity on the dating websites at this time of year. No-one wants to be alone and unloved at Christmas. And for some guys having a partner for a few weeks made the loneliness of the rest of the year bearable. This was the time to catch the gullible, vulnerable guys.

The crowds were sparse on Grafton Street once you moved away from the entrance of the St.Stephens Green Centre. It had once been the bustling shopping street of the capital but a rash of newly built shopping centers in the suburbs had sealed its fate.

The famous "Bewley's" coffee house, once the second home to some of Dublin's finest artists, writers, musicians and the elite of Dublin society felt abandoned, like its cultural heart had been ripped out. Its many seats, light dappled by the Harry Clarke stained windows lay idle in an eerie jeweled light.

The odd one or two couples — sipping coffee more to shelter from the weather than appreciate the craftsmanship of the décor or to soak up some of its historical atmosphere, gave the place no atmosphere or ambient chatter at all. There was no pleasure in sitting in silence in an almost empty room. Sophie abandoned her half drunken latte on the table and left, braving the icy punch of cold air at the mahogany double doors.

The sleet spattered cobbles outside were gritty and uneven under her cold, damp feet. An occasional busker or hawker broke the monotony of the mostly deserted street.

Once glorious and expensive shops crammed this street, now they lay idle, closed, windows dark except for gaudy auctioneers signs. Most of the big names were reeling, punch drunk by the recession, hampered by the crippling, spiraling rents and ever increasing parking fees and fines, many had defected to the suburban shopping centre's or not survived at all.

Undeterred by weather or economics, the tough women manning the flower stalls still braved the elements. Generations of hard work and battering by the Irish climate made these women impenetrable to anything. It was a welcome sight to see them, these tough women, still there, brightening up the drab street with stalls jam packed with bright blooms and the women themselves colouring the quiet street with their language.

Sophie had fond memories of being brought shopping here as a child, each shop competing, Irish owned for the most part, constantly outdoing each other with their window displays; but for every child in Ireland the ultimate was to be brought to Grafton Street; some came on a day trip from all corners of the island just to see the Christmas window display in Switzers department store.

The lucky ones got in line for a visit to see Santa afterwards and wore a badge with pride declaring that fact. It was here that parents who couldn't afford to shop in Switzers could claim a little of the magic to give to their children for free – the window.

Children were jostled past reluctant strangers' legs to the front, through the scratchy curtains of long gabardines and rain Macs, hauled up on their fathers' rain soaked shoulders just to catch a glimpse through the bustling, noisy crowds at the winter wonderland scenes behind the glass. Happy childhood memories were made of sodden woolen coats, freezing noses and cigarette smoke, twinkling lights, moving window displays all set to the backdrop of the cheerful street decorations and carols sung by enthusiastic choirs further up the street, each shaking jingling buckets of coppers and spare change.

That time had passed for Dublin and for modern kids. Now the child-friendly winter scenes had been replaced by lifelike "size zero" mannequins decked out in the expensive designer gear available in the store; no sign of Santa, his elves workshop, or even a layer of fake aero bead snow. Sophie thought how sad it was for the lack of it, it wasn't even Switzers anymore, it had been swallowed up and digested by a bigger department store. Something vital and friendly had been lost to the city, or in reality had been discarded by modernity.

It seemed Grafton Street itself had been dissolved and diluted down. The bespoke shops offering unique goods were gone, to be replaced by the breed of shops found on any high street in the U.K., Clothes shops were stuffed with goods from Bangladeshi sweatshops, they had spread like measles.

The jewelers were a constant though, particularly "Weirs" commanding the whole corner. It was impossible to pass the glittering and impossibly beautiful window displays of diamonds and other treasures. Occasional couples paused giggling before the windows, faces illuminated, banter and nudges to the ribs before moving off with nervous laughter, leaving the window free to throw its sparkling spell to a couple that may be serious about buying an engagement ring, just as her parents had from there.

Sophie found herself outside Trinity College, she had daydreamed and angrily sleep walked all the way down to its wrought iron railings. Her parents had studied here, and as a child she had often been brought around the hallowed buildings. It was the best Ireland had to offer; it was beloved, adored and respected and had seen some of the world's greatest talents through their education and beyond. Here the "Book of Kells" rested, that beautiful work of monastic art visited by travelers from across the globe yet for the most part ignored by the Irish themselves. She stood and took in the scale and magnificence of the stone façade, an imposing beauty broken by the famous archway and double wooden doors, once closed to all except the distinguished and privileged few. She considered wandering in but looked up at the leaden sky pregnant with more sleet and hail, it was time to head for home and get ready for tonight.

It had been a mostly wasted trip, all it had done was make her mood depressed, the happy childhood memories of shopping here at Christmas were gone forever, they could never be re-created.

The heart of the place was dead despite the shops valiant efforts with loud pop music and gaudy signs. The famous figures of the street were gone —street performers and mime artists like "the Dice man" made the place sadder by their absence.

Groups of Roma gypsies were dotted on the street corners, begging with their drugged babies swaddled in filthy blankets. In doorways homeless guys were cocooned in their sleeping bags, empty beer cans and hamburger boxes strewn at their feet.

A choir halfheartedly singing carols for charity seemed the only genuine and good thing here. The atmosphere was gone; it pissed her off that the vital essence that had made her childhood memories had expired. This new Grafton Street was a bland, soul-less decaying street with half empty shops.

As a teenager she could remember being allowed "come into town" with her school friends. They always sat upstairs and at the front of the green double Decker; famous bus number "46A", windows fogged up and streaming condensation from damp anoraks, smelly

PVC seats, chattering women blowing clouds of cigarette smoke while dandling toddlers on their laps, sharing a joke or some gossip with the satchel wearing conductor, armed with his hand cranked ticket machine.

Hours were spent wandering from shop to shop, taking it all in, the glorious, noisy, smelly atmosphere of the vibrant, penniless Dublin before the Celtic tiger and the boom that destroyed it.

Every café was busy, all offered homemade food as a default setting and she and her giddy friends would pool their money to eat like kings, in modest places like "The Bad Ass Café", it seemed now all that was on offer was the disappointing offerings of factory made cupcakes and rip off Panini's.

In those halcyon days Temple bar was a crumbling, bohemian Mecca, perfect for browsing through shops crammed full of second hand clothes, record shops, crammed antique shops and brick a brack from the flea market.

Whole days were spent leisurely wandering when Dublin was at its best and safest. This was Temple bar long before the gastro pubs, stag nights and expensive apartments.

Looking around Dublin now and it was impossible to ignore the invasion of professional beggars, wino's, junkies and pick pockets roaming in small herds, undeterred by the occasional bored looking and outnumbered Gardai. It was almost Dickensian.

It seemed every second voice passing her was foreign – eastern European or Polish and she couldn't help but grind her teeth. The innocent babbling of the foreigners ignited something deep and hateful in her, she wanted them to fuck off and leave, she had no time for these "new Irish", they were replacing the familiar voices and faces she was used to, breeding like rabbits and sucking the social welfare dry in her eyes. She hadn't expected so many of them to be out and about on Grafton street, she realised she had been biting the inside of her cheek when she tasted the metallic tang of blood.

She paid her parking at the vending machine and stormed back to her car, she would never visit Grafton Street again. A wave of melancholy washed over her, her childhood memories and familiar places had always acted like an anchor for her but they were slowly eroding away.

She had an unexplainable sadness at the loss of the Ireland of her youth, it was wrecked, irreplaceable characters and shops were gone, there was only one way to lift this feeling and she hoped her date tonight would give her that release.

CHAPTER 15

She managed to get a parking space on the main road, just slightly down from the pub where she was to meet him. A quick check of her make-up and a squirt of perfume and she was ready.

She knew the attached car park had CCTV but there were no cameras trained on this side of the street, it allowed her linger, savour a cigarette and go over her plan, checking for hazards.

She pulled her hat lower as she walked in the main door, she had been here before and had noted the camera placements, this was not the type of pub she was comfortable with. It was "well to do" south inner city, Ballsbridge was the embassy belt. Its pubs were bustling; the type of place close to town where people sat watching the door in case someone famous came in, it was also frequented by the rugby types being so close to the posh new stadium. It attracted the well heeled groups for pre dinner drinks before gorging themselves in the popular Michelin starred restaurant next door.

She spotted him sitting at a low table with another guy, not a good start if he had friends in the pub. She gave him a wave to get his attention then turned away so his companion wouldn't see her face. He made his way over grinning, through the groups of twos and threes glued to the rugby on the big screen, pint glasses held tight to the chest.

They exchanged the usual nervous pleasantries, until he mentioned his friend, — an old school pal he'd just bumped into and "was it ok to watch the rugby and his friend to join them?" Bollox, this was not going well, and it was best to abandon it. "Eh no, actually, I don't do double dates, I just wouldn't be comfortable with that to be honest". As soon as she said that his face changed from smiling to sheer contempt. His eyes were hooded and he shrugged, made a sucking noise through his teeth and stuck out his hand to shake hers, like she was a guy. She noticed his wedding ring and he realised she had seen it. "Are you taking the piss?" she spat, he took a step back in mock disgust. "Give me a break, for fucks sake, what's the big deal, you're looking for a ride same as me yeah?"

He stood there indignant but angry, bristling in his Leinster rugby top as if she had mortally wounded him, she felt like throwing up on his precious rugby top. Without a second glance he turned on his heels and made his way back to his friend. What a waste of time and effort! A missed opportunity, all that preparation and all for what? A total selfish dickhead looking for some action off-side while wifey sits at home.

He deserved more than food poisoning for this. She had a three day plan and had booked time off work for him.

Sophie turned on her heels and made for the door, looking back once, and through a gap in the crowd saw him give a high five and clink pint glasses with his drinking buddy.

This one would be revisited and he would pay for that little display of arrogance and chauvinism.

To the side of the pub was a stone archway leading into a dark, dingy alley. This stinking narrow cavern was used by the pub and restaurant for their bins and deliveries, it was also where some people gathered to light up since the smoking ban, some went there to piss, others to grope and shag out of the glare of the street lights, not very romantic amongst the beer kegs, rotten vegetable scraps and cigarette ends.

She watched him lumber drunkenly out of the pub alone. He leaned against the jamb of the door to steady himself, scuffing his shoulder along the wall, the guy was buckled with drink, she locked her gaze on him as he fumbled in his pockets and pull out a crumpled cigarette from a bashed box, and after a few attempts he finally got it lighting. He was dragging hard on it as he lumbered his way to the alley to piss.

She sprang from her car and shot across the street dodging the traffic, tip toeing down the alley towards his shadowy profile, and the sound of forceful splashing against the wall.

The acrid smell of piss ignited her rage, her nostrils flared and she gritted her teeth. There he was, the male buck who had fucked up her plans for him, one arm leaning on the wall, head down, cigarette in mouth, holding his dick, splashing his piss all over the wall and the leg of his trousers.

She stepped around the meandering stream of piss and got behind him, her soft ballet pumps masking the sound of her footsteps. She plunged the syringe into his neck and jumped back into the shadows, flattening herself against the wall, he spun around, dick hanging out of his trousers trying to register what had happened, swatting blindly at his neck. He was blinking fast and the cigarette fell from his lips, hissing in defiance as it went out in his piss.

She picked up the needle, capped it and slid it into her coat pocket. She waited a few seconds before gently walking towards him. "Shit, are you ok? I saw what that guy did to you" she said with concern. "Here, let me help you", he had no idea this was the same girl as earlier, she adopted a soft country accent, she wore different clothes, wig and make-up.

He was heavy, but she got in under his stinking armpit and levered him, with her free hand she shoved his dick back into his trousers, disgusted that his piss was now on her hands. He didn't refuse her help instead he doubled over to vomit all down the front of his beloved Leinster shirt; she kept him moving all the way to her car. Drivers felt sorry for her and slowed to let her cross. Not one person passing her batted an eyelid, just another drunk being brought home after the rugby by his girlfriend.

As soon as he was in the passenger seat he was unconscious. She put the passenger seat on full recline and slammed the door on him. Her efforts weren't wasted after all.

At the next red light the stink of his vomit overcame her, it pooled around her like a stinking fog without the breeze coming in to dilute it, she retched, a physical response she despised as she had no control over it.

She fumbled under her seat while keeping one eye on the lights and anyone around, her fingertips griped a claw hammer wrapped in newspaper, she gently draped the newspaper over his face and smashed the claw hammer with force onto the bump where his nose was, again, and again she smashed his nose to a bloody pulp under the paper, her blows only limited by the headspace in the car. Her tenderizing leaving a gaping hole in the middle of his face, the flesh that was his nose hung in limp ribbons and tatters across his cheeks, it smeared onto the newspaper like the guts of a squashed bug, how DARE he stink up her car with vomit! What she would do to him for messing her around tonight would be a whole lot worse.

The muscles in her shoulders relaxed and she could feel her stress lifting, she could just open the door now, push him out and leave him in a crumpled heap on the road, she could drive home with a smile on her face knowing his carousing days were over, but where's the fun in that?

"The buck" started to come around in the bath; he was stupefied, sluggish and confused from the drugs and cold water. Ice cubes bobbed alongside his naked hairy body. His wrists and ankles were secured by three cable ties. He was a big fucker and she wasn't taking any chances of him trying to overpower her.

The gag was cutting into the corners of his mouth and his gums were dry and sore from exposure. His breathing had been hampered by his smashed in nose so Sophie had hacked away the fleshy tatters to ease his breathing, exposing the two red nasal passages.

She sat naked on the edge of the bath watching him try to make sense of his situation. She was cursing him for being so heavy, her lower back was aching, and she was raging with herself for being rash and deviating from her normally military like planning. She should have pitched him out on the road.

Wide eyed fear and panic was setting in and he started thrashing wildly, sloshing water and ice all over the bathroom floor. "I don't think I like what you're doing" she said calmly. Her voice startled him, and his fear turned to instant hatred when he recognised her. He mumbled something through the gag at her which she ignored; she knew he was cursing her out. It was to be expected at this stage.

She picked up a little silver hand mirror her grandmother had left her and put it to him to show him the ruin of his face. He screamed through the gag, tears streaming down his face, eyes imploring her, he pissed and shit in the bath from fear. "It's as clear as the nose on your face that you —my friend, are a lying, cheating, disrespectful prick." Sophie put her hand to her mouth mocking him, then said "oh dear, you HAVE no nose, poor fucker" his tethered body thrashed from side to side, his hampered mouth tried to scream then his eyes locked on her, she was standing up and let the head of the hammer slide from her palm and gripped the handle as it slid through her fingers coming to rest beside her smooth naked thigh.

This deliberate act was to heighten his fear and let him see what was coming next. "Do you remember that mad film where the woman broke the guy's ankles? Misery —that's it, great film" he looked down the length of his naked body and realized not only were his ankles strapped but there was a wooden board under the soles of his feet and behind that a rolled up towel all held on by strips of heavy duty duct tape.

He was still looking at his feet when she smashed the hammer down on the ridge of his ugly left foot; with hardly a pause she smashed his right foot. He was screaming and choking with the pain and his shocked body was rigid, pain tortured eyes rolling in their sockets.

She lifted a little blue and silver tube from the sink, grabbed a handful of his hair to steady him and squirted the contents of the tube all over the gag. She super glued his mouth, entombing him and his swearing behind the gag forever, his tongue caught on the glue and his mouth filled with blood as his flesh ripped trying to free himself to scream.

He passed out for a few minutes and woke up weaker and quieter than before, she hated when the pain kicked in and overcame them, they lost their fight and didn't concentrate on what she was saying or doing to them, it enraged her.

She took a sip of her well deserved wine, her favorite, an expensive "Chateau neuf du Pape". Reverently, she set down the Waterford crystal glass, part of a gift set from her parents, on the sink. She brushed down her bare breasts as if shaking off crumbs, rubbed her palms together and said, "Right, where were we?"

She grabbed fistfuls of his hair in both hands and pulled and tugged at it with all her strength, nearly bodily dragging him from the bath until she felt the scalp come loose finally on his skull. She dropped him back down into the fouled icy water. With the precision of a butcher she slit the skin on his forehead, grabbed the ripped piece and hacked and peeled it back off his skull. She turned the overhead shower on to scalding hot and marveled as the slimy skull revealed itself like an ostrich egg, creamy and gleaming. Pink, slimy blood ran down his shell shocked face.

His eyes were rolling in his head again as she turned off the shower. She needed to work quickly now, keep him awake. She grabbed the small garden secateurs from the sink and lifted his left hand, splaying his fingers to expose the wedding ring finger, opened the shears and the blades bit in on either side of the offending digit, he suddenly grabbed at her hands and dug his nails into her knuckle, raking the skin. She pulled back, free from his grip and turned on the tap in the sink, she rinsed her torn bleeding knuckle and examined it under the light, it irritated her but wouldn't hamper her. She raised her glass and took a greedy gulp of her wine. She toasted his little useless attack.

In two determined strides she was leaning over the bath and glaring at him. Like eagles claws she hooked his finger again, the blades bit into the flesh, scuffing the wedding ring, with both hands squeezing the arms of the secateurs together she pulled back from him with all her might. Like the finger of a glove, his flesh easily peeled off exposing the long white, knobbled finger bone, only catching as the fingernail tore away. She leaned her ass against the cool ceramic of the washbasin, leisurely picking the flesh away from the blades to get to the blood smeared ring tangled in the gory mess, she rinsed it under the running water and held the glittering gold up to the light as if examining an exquisite diamond, before slamming it down beside the soap. "You won't need this again pal"

His body was convulsing in the water, arms failing up and down in pain, bright blood spurting from his finger, cascading in the air like a sporadic fountain splashing back down onto his face.

He finally slowed, relaxed, and started to slump in the water, bloody bubbles formed and popped from the two nasal cavities in his face. He glared at her through his pain and the stubborn hate in his eyes enraged her.

She picked up the hammer from the toilet seat and smashed him on the side of the head above his ear like a Wimbledon champion. Her mother's hard earned cash on tennis lessons had served her well. The side of his skull collapsed in a jelly like concavity, sharp bones threatened to poke through the pulverized skin. He slumped down under the filthy water as a snake of blood made a slow meander from his ear and nose cavities, his eyes, bulging and purple black from the hemorrhage of the blow, he reminded her one of those religious statues weeping blood that dotted the corridors of her old school, a tear of blood trickled down his cheek from his crushed eye orbit into the filthy water. this was not a satisfying end for her, she now needed to finish the job and get rid of him. She had a glass of wine waiting. This fucker had robbed her, he hadn't shown the usual pleading, the imploring eyes, not that it would have saved him anyway, but he had robbed her of satisfaction. He was a tough fucker to the end. The Bastard.

She yanked the plug to drain the filthy water, dragging a plastic sheet from behind over her head, and leaned over the bath making a tent, in that close, intimate space with the buck she slowly and carefully make a nick with the Stanley blade on his femoral and carotid arteries, her breasts brushing his face and flaccid groin as she worked, the ends of her hair blood soaked and congealing, globs of bloody clots clinging to her breasts. She slashed sharply into the inside of his thick upper thighs to speed things up, the carpet knife raking and rasping through the thick layers of skin, catching in the flesh, her hands were sticky and slippery with his blood.

Squirts of warm pulsing blood splashed her face and breasts as a final act of defiance, he may as well have been spitting in her face, when the worst of the spurting had passed she opened the veins in his wrists and turned the shower on again to warm him up and wash the wine red blood down the drain.

The buck was going into seizure from the blood loss and she just hoped his heart would beat long enough to get the job done.

Viciously she slashed the blade across the base of his neck on both sides, the job made easier by his seizure forcing the arteries and veins in his neck to stand proud, she severed the tendons and muscles so that his head flopped loosely from side to side, resting awkwardly on his chest. The blood gurgled and welled out in a steady lazy flow from under his chin and cascaded down his hairy chest. Bloody bubbles pooled under his chin as the last of his breath pushed through the ebbing flow.

She threw the plastic sheet into her walk in shower and rinsed it down while he bled his last in the bath. Once he was dead she opened the window and put on the extractor fan, she made a c-section slash across his abdomen to release the body fluids and pull out the intestines. With venom she slashed at it to release the shit and digested food and washed it away with the shower water, this was like cleaning tripe and it was the part she hated.

The smell was rancid, vile and overpowering but she had put on a dust mask smeared on "Vicks" to make it bearable, within an hour he was drained and cleared out, ready to be dissected and disposed of. Thanks to the weekend butchery course she had taken in a country boutique hotel it wouldn't be a problem, just exhausting.

Limbs and torso were wrapped in towels and three sturdy garden waste bags for transportation; she always removed these and disposed of them separately. The towels always made their way to some clothes bank or other.

The head was always the last thing she tackled as she preferred to deal with it in the kitchen at the sink or the breakfast counter. The job of de-fleshing and removing the teeth was time consuming and needed a large pot of coffee and a cigarette. Her wine had lost its appeal.

After four hours the buck was parceled up into twelve separate pieces, all neatly and securely leak-proof. His internal organs rested in a bucket. She fished out different organs and made batches of slush in her food processor, she flushed them down the toilet in small batches every hour with a pint of bleach, this wasn't something she did all the time but she just wanted this bastard gone. She put his head in a plastic storage box and carried it through to the kitchen once the coffee was ready.

On her breakfast counter sat a roasting tin with a large central spike for securing the roast. She lifted his head out of the Perspex box and forced it down onto the spike and twisted it from side to side until she was happy it was secure.

She stood back and took in the ruin that was the bucks head, the temple was caved in, the battered flesh turning purple, his scalp was bare and the bone of the skull had lost its former sheen, the edges of his nasal cavity were also drying and looking like cured meat. Those eyes, which were so full of hate right to the end, already milky over purple, and visibly shrunken; that vital spark of life long gone. Gone with it, his "fuck you" hateful resistance.

She grabbed a hold of the loose flap of hair still clinging to his head and hacked it off, placing it carefully in a plastic bag, —a free hair transplant for Ger? She smirked to herself. She slashed away the glue encrusted gag with the sticky Stanley blade, taking lumps of flesh with it.

She made deep slashes up either side of the ruined mouth as far as his cheek bones to widen it and stuck her left hand in, holding the bottom teeth and tongue down, and with her right hand twisted at an awkward angle, gripped his top teeth and roof of his mouth with her fingertips, digging her nails into the flesh inside his mouth for grip.

It took a few minutes of serious effort to lever the jaws apart. Finally she felt the muscles and ligaments give way with a sickly wet crack, that sound always reminded her of her father tearing the leg from the Christmas turkey, the top part of his skull tilted back to expose the whole inside of his mouth, the bottom jaw hung loosely in its skin. Dark grey fillings dotted his cigarette stained teeth.

Sophie's pliers would do the job of removing the teeth but first she had to loosen them in the skull, she'd had enough of this guy for one day.

She wrapped the head in tin foil and placed it in the oven on a low heat, this was just like cooking a leg of lamb to her, though she'd never eat this shit. She'd gotten a recipe for slow cooked fillet of pork from a friend's website, a childhood pal from Dublin who now ran a thriving, popular restaurant in the tourist Mecca of Kerry, yep, "Treyvaud's" could certainly knock out some good cooking tips, though she doubted Paul ever had this in mind.

The smell was no different to roast pork once the flesh started to cook, she placed chopped onions, apples and herbs in the roasting dish with some chicken stock. This was nothing like the acrid vomit inducing smell of flesh that Hollywood would have you believe. It was sweet, and wouldn't alert the neighbours. Just as she was balancing the dish on the lip of the oven she remembered! Laughing to herself she had a quick scrabble in the drawer and got it, a wooden bamboo skewer, normally used for kebab or satay, but in this case it was to avoid the gun shot pop of eyeballs during the night. She had nightmares for weeks the last time it happened. A quick skewer of the eyes to release the pressure and jelly guaranteed no bang in the oven, and no leaping out of bed with fright.

She cleaned up the bathroom like a professional forensic cleaner, bleaching and scrubbing the tiles before finally stepping into her shower.

The scalding water did nothing to relieve the sheer exhaustion she felt, she rolled her shoulders and stretched, the clots of blood rolling down her body like gorged leeches, doing some yoga moves to try and loosen up her sore tired muscles, a sharp jolt of pain in her lower back told her she had done too much. She had rushed this, had taken a risk, and it pissed her off.

She would dispose of the buck the next day but first she needed sleep. Her head was swimming with exhaustion. As his head slow roasted in the oven she checked over her parcels in the bathroom, rolling them like kneaded dough to check for leaks, she had been hasty before and had paid the price when fluid had oozed in the boot of her car, the garage had ripped her off with the price of that new boot carpet, she didn't intend getting caught out again. Again and again she went over the path to the kitchen with a baby wipe then scalded the tiles with her steam cleaner just in case a stray clot of blood had eluded her, or was hiding under the kitchen presses, before finally climbing into bed as the dawn chorus began, she gratefully closed her eyes for an unsatisfying sleep.

Outside the people of Dublin were waking to another pre-Christmas winter's day.

No doubt the buck's wife would put his absence from their marital bed down to another hard nights drinking and womanising. It would most likely be a situation she was used to, and would buy Sophie time to dispose of him before the missing persons report was filed.

It would be days before his photo on the "missing persons in Ireland" Facebook page would feature his photo and description.

What a waste of a few days leave from the office, fuck it, she thought, may as well get back to the grind, she could always take the few days again if she needed to, and she was due plenty. She hadn't taken a summer holiday in a few years, unlike some of her colleagues who wasted the year looking forward to two weeks of sunshine and frolics.

CHAPTER 16

Another Monday morning and her bathroom sparkled as always, nothing was out of place in her apartment.

The filthy weather over the weekend had allowed her to dispose of the buck without any human contact in either the remote bog holes or lesser known forestry she chose. Not even the weather hardened hill-walkers would venture out in that squall.

She had nearly lost it in the car a few times, the tyres slid and pirouetted on the ice but she controlled the revs and steered, avoiding the brakes and keeping her gears low. It wouldn't be funny to be discovered with a dismembered body in the boot by being stupid and crashing the car into a ditch. That advanced driving course at Mondello race track had come in handy after all; it was one of the better birthday presents from her sister.

The Dublin Mountains stood sentinel over the ever expanding city and suburbs. It really was a city trapped between the mountains and the sea. It meant that everyone below was blasted by the arctic chill that had dusted the distant mountaintops with early snow.

Commuters muffled their chins at bus stops and resigned themselves to being pelted by the frigid sleet creeping its way down across the city. Thrill seekers with four by four's were already setting Facebook and twitter alight with their exploits; some relished the danger in braving the winter's first snow. Mountain rescue teams were kept busy rescuing these foolhardy idiots and the occasional walker caught out by the deteriorating conditions, it was a treat for the thrill seekers and families alike, throwing a few snowballs and decorating a lone fir tree with surplus Christmas decorations before coming back down to the reality of the more temperate suburbs below.

It wasn't the best conditions for Sophie. Her car was a rear wheel drive designed for city streets and motorways, not hazardous, rutted and slippery mountain roads. It meant she would have to curtail her activities until the weather improved. She had considered buying a four by four, something robust like a Land Rover Defender, the ultimate go anywhere workhorse but on reflection she knew people would ask dumb questions as to why she would drive something like that when she lived in an apartment in the city, it would attract too much attention.

The thought had crossed her mind of maybe renting a more rural property, not too remote but just enough privacy and land to continue her interests. But the thought of being isolated and vulnerable, even for someone like her ruled it out. There was safety in numbers as a woman; she wasn't so naïve to think she was invulnerable; the odds were only in her favour when she controlled the situation, so her apartment with private lift was suitable for the time being, apart from anything else, the commute would be a bitch.

The slow grind of Dublin city centre traffic allowed her mind to drift and recall her first kill as her windscreen wipers beat a slow tattoo across the sleet spattered screen. Tropical heat from the fan gave two fingers to the arctic chill pummeling her car.

In the foothills of the Dublin Mountains lay a sprawling suburb of, for the most part, social housing. The development bred nasty little gangsters and tribes of teenage mothers. It was an up and coming "Hoodie" she had cut her teeth on at the tender age of nineteen.

She had watched him and his gang for days, parking at the top of the road where he lived and hung out, she had sat in her battered "first car" watching him as he bought chips, booze and drugs in his local area.

He seemed popular with the teenagers, a modern day hero to the dysfunctional future criminals of the area. She had sat and watched kids delight in his recognition of their cat called congratulations, smiling with religious fervour at his benevolence. He had recently been released from Wheatfield prison, a notorious breeding ground for Dublin's criminals.

She had sat quietly with her window down listening to him and his mates make plans for the weekend.

She parked her car facing the entrance to the nightclub and strolled confidently past the bouncers, she mingled with the crowd and kept her head down to avoid the CCTV at the entrance.

A crowd of women she could blend in with were gathered in a corner, her stomach had butterflies and her head was giddy with anxiety and anticipation. She had gone over a number of scenarios in her head and of course all the escape routes and exits.

The group of women she picked to align herself with were on a hen night, each festooned with feather boas, sparkly cowboy hats, and plastic penis necklaces. Their accent gave them away immediately, they were from "down the country" or one of Ireland rural towns, they hadn't done their homework on the cheap hotel next door or else they would have known the reputation for this nightclub and shabby area. Had they know "the form" of this area and the patrons they would have been more subdued, in fact terrified. They were innocents in a dodgy area, where the girls in this nightclub wouldn't think twice about shoving a glass in their ruddy country cheeks.

Sophie hovered at the edge of the group and then spotted the notorious "Wayne". She hung back and watched for ten minutes, nobody in the nightclub took any notice of her. His image flitted through the gaps in the crowd so she moved forward and turned sideways offering a good view of her ass when he looked over.

His gang of about eight track-suit wearing Yobs were congratulating him and toasting his early release from prison. His latest spell in prison was for beating up an elderly shop keeper; unacceptably late with his protection money.

Wayne was a product of his environment, tough neighborhoods' where stray dogs roamed and sometimes ended up tortured or on a bonfire for laughs, feral kids and rubbish dumped in the Street was their normal. Joy riding and burning out cars kept the teenagers busy at weekends.

He was a tough looking guy, early twenties, but on borrowed time, prison tats, tracksuit and shaved head. Definitely a guy you would cross the road to avoid, but Sophie wanted him.

He was living the Dublin gangster lifestyle, constantly hassled by the police, partying hard and snorting coke like a pig, breaking jaws and waiting for that inevitable bullet with his name on it.

Sophie hovered closer to his crowd, this was the dangerous time, if any of the slappers in Wayne's party took offence, or thought she was moving in on one of their crowd this would end violently for Sophie.

He spotted her and she allowed the eye contact to linger, he was intrigued, she gave a demure smile then looked down and away. Within a minute he was behind her sliding his rough calloused hands up the back of her skirt and gripping her ass cheek, she could feel his sharp finger nails bite into the soft flesh of her ass but she didn't flinch.

Sophie slowly turned towards him and tipped her chin towards the exit, gripped his hand and led him away from his crowd. She threaded her way through the crowd leading him, deliberately exaggerating the roll of her hips and tightened her ass as she walked, she couldn't allow him to get distracted before he was outside.

Her pulse was drumming in her ears competing with the loud dance music pumping in the club, her body was awash with adrenaline, and she felt bile rising in her throat, she fought the urge to gag and pushed through to the double doors, head down past the bouncers and across the car-park. They didn't take any notice, she was just another slapper going outside for a quick ride, and they saw it all the time.

Wayne never questioned or spoke, Sophie hit the remote button on her car and unquestioningly he got in. before she slid into the driver's seat she did a quick mental run through of her plan for Wayne.

She flicked on the headlights facing the doors so that anyone looking over wouldn't see the car's occupants or the registration plate.

With coquettish smile she produced a silver hip flask from the side pocket of her door and offered it to him; without hesitation he threw his greasy head back and swallowed hard, his Adams apple bobbed up and down as he emptied the flask not even offering her some. Wayne relaxed back in the passenger seat and put his hands behind his head and made it obvious that she had to do all the work.

Her hands trembled as she leaned over and pulled at his tracksuit bottoms to get to his groin, she had prepared herself for this, this act was simply to distract him while the sedative kicked in, she fumbled with the tie string and elastic top until finally she pulled his dick free. She began to slowly mouth up and down his shaft listening to his breathing as she worked, his groin stank of salty sweat and his cock tasted sour and putrid with piss, it tasted rank, she had to concentrate on not gagging as the smell of him filled her nostrils.

He twisted his fingers into the delicate cat hairs at the nape of her neck and forcefully moved her harder and faster on his cock, the effort not to gag was monumental but she squeezed her eyes tight and started a countdown. She had to appear compliant.

His fingers started to loosen in her hair and his dick was losing its aggression and was going soft in her mouth. She spat out his stinking cock, and sat back in her seat watching him.

He was almost paralysed but yet managed to slur "fucking cunt, spike me fuckin drink" before lunging for her and falling forward to smash his face on the steering wheel and land in her lap. Sophie grabbed his tracksuit top and shoved him back in his seat. She leaned across him, he was powerless to resist but the burning hate in his eyes weren't dimmed by the sedative. She spat the taste of his putrid cock into his face in a spray. She lay across him and buzzed the electric button on the side of his seat to fully recline; she sat back and lit a well earned cigarette, drawing hard on it to get the taste of him out of her mouth.

Within minutes all trace of her and Wayne ever being there were gone. The Gardai put out a half hearted appeal for "The public's help in tracing the whereabouts of Wayne Doherty who was known to the Gardai". In true Irish fashion once the "known to Gardai" bit was heard nobody cared, they switched off; it was assumed that Wayne was picked off by a rival gang.

In Dublin gangland he wasn't missed for long and the next gangster moved up to fill the vacuum. Sophie could even recall a rumour that the IRA had been responsible for his disappearance over a drug debt. How convenient. That was her first successful but very amateur abduction.

Wayne had been disposed of in a very haphazard, bloody and messy manner that night. Through experience Sophie had learned to leave no loose ends, never dismember at the dump site, but she went against all the golden rules for serial killers and revisited the site. She moved his stinking bones two years later to a more secluded area and reburied them; she brought branches of a yew tree from a local graveyard in a bin bag. The Yew trees are poisonous, and avoided by animals that might feel the urge to burrow near the grave.

She could remember the gut swooping shot of adrenaline and panic when she heard a news report that a body had been found by forestry workers, the reports said it was near the scenic car park on mount Venus road where she buried him.

She could recall clearly the lunchtime news bulletin and the icy grip of fear that grabbed and twisted her guts, the people and noises around her became distant and muffled, her head swam with dizziness. She got a hold of herself and recounted all of her precautions, all her efforts to avoid DNA transference.

She had never been questioned by the Gardai; they were unable to identify the female seen leaving with Wayne that night. She had never been to court or even got a parking ticket, she was fastidious about staying under the radar.

Her preparation for Wayne's kill had been text book but amatuer. She had read everything she could find on serial killers and tried to learn from their mistakes. There would be no fingerprints as she wore three layers of gloves, she had shaved away all her body hair; and when she buried Wayne she was naked except for the scant protection of the Tyvec paper suit her father had bought her from "Woodie's DIY" to "save her clothes when painting her room". Wearing a latex swimming hat had been a nightmare, it pulled at her scalp. She traded her car in the following week for a newer car under the governments "Scrappage Scheme", terrified that any trace of him remained, and also because the car was on its last legs anyway, her father kindly acted as guarantor on the only loan she ever indulged in. She was utterly self sufficient these days.

These days she could dismember and wrap victims in the comfort of her own comfortable and thankfully, heated bathroom without braving the elements in her skin. Time, knowledge and experience had made her a professional disposal expert.

CHAPTER 17

Sophie ramped up her meetings with Greta and started to notice a change in her, there was a new confidence to her and she was wearing more make-up, gone was the thick band of leaden grey in her hairline, she was having her hair done. It was all to impress Sophie.

She realised though that there was a fine line between building up someone's confidence to manipulate them and then over doing it, creating an unmanageable and overconfident monster.

Like a professional but unethical psychologist Sophie drew and re-drew the fine line until Greta was outwardly happy but still pliable and open to suggestion, she had complimented her then sown seeds of doubt easily. She had watched the "Hannibal" series enough times to see manipulation and subliminal suggestion at work.

On Sophie's suggestion a girly shopping trip was organised, a carefully chosen boutique in the quaint seaside village of Dalkey. The type of place where nice upper middle class people live, old money, the odd ageing rockstar; happily sitting in his pile, content that tourists have their picture taken outside their gate; adding to their sense of importance and relevance. For some reason it also attracted film directors, a reclusive singer living like Rapunzel in her turreted castle, and the odd retired formula one driver all jostling for the best and most exclusive position in this enclave overlooking the Sorrento like bay.

The beautiful people sat sipping lattes outside the overpriced cafés. It was the home of eccentricity with money. It boasted the most expensive houses in Ireland, particularly those fortunate to have the sea view overlooking Dalkey Island and its monastic ruin.

The boutique chosen by Sophie was perfect. It was an exclusive shop, by appointment only, and accessed by a buzzer and locked door. It played up to Greta's sense of entitlement and importance. Sophie knew it well as her mother's GP surgery was just a few doors down.

The female sales assistants did all the hard work for Sophie, kiss-assing to Greta, telling her each outfit was made for her, their greedy manicured claws only interested in getting hold of her credit card and a fat commission.

Sophie deliberately herded her towards outfits designed with the younger woman in mind, hesitant at first, reluctant to try anything new, then goaded on by the vampyric sales women, she passed over her credit card. She even wore a new outfit out of the shop to the café next door.

The tight Jodhpur leggings, sleeveless top and short denim jacket did no favours to her and made no improvement to Greta's middle aged figure.

She sipped her coffee self consciously under the giant patio heater, tugging at the new and unforgiving top to pull it further over her rounded pot belly. It was only a tip inducing compliment from the sleazy waiter that stopped her heading for the toilets to change back into her dowdy clothes.

It seemed a compliment from a slimy waiter held more weight than the previous hour's sucking up from the sales assistants and Sophie. This was the measure of the woman and it made Sophie despise her even more.

It pleased Sophie no end to know that Greta would be dealt a double blow to her confidence when she went home, enough to wipe the smug grin off her face courtesy of her own husband.

It was utterly predictable that he would go crazy when he saw the clothes; odds were he would say something unflattering, insulting and patronising. A row would ensue; Greta, buoyed by fake compliments would defend her choices and both would storm off. That is, until he checked his online credit card statement and realise just how much she had spent, and predictably kick off round two.

All of this played perfectly into Sophie's hand, who better to offer support, understanding and a shoulder to cry on than Sophie?

Over the past few weeks she had carefully and masterfully fed the woman's confidence and self esteem, evening walks on Dun Laoghaire pier followed by an ice cream from the famous "Teddys", weekend trips to farmers markets in Marley Park, all with lots of coffee, cigarettes and girly jokes thrown in. Sophie hated every minute of it but it was having the effect she wanted —she was now indispensible. She seemed to be the only person capable of rescuing the woman from abject misery.

CHAPTER 18

Flyers were up in various places near the office for an ABBA tribute night; Sophie was not a fan of their music unlike her sister and mother.

The fact that this night was organised by the gay alliance and "The lesbians of Dublin association" worked perfectly, a girl only night; unless, you included drag queens.

Greta jumped at the suggestion of a girly night, and an ABBA night-even better! Sophie omitted to tell her it would be jam packed full of lesbians and drag artists.

The woman was like a hyper teenager full of "Red bull" bouncing into the taxi when Sophie picked her up, she flopped into the back seat clutching her bag to her chest, the smell of cigarettes and wine followed her and fogged up the car. She defiantly wore one of her new outfits and had most likely, the best part of a bottle of wine while waiting for the taxi.

She yapped all the way into the city centre, giddy and a total pain in the ass.

Sophie had made a few calls and a generous cash donation thanks to "The Bucks" wallet towards the lesbian charity and this afforded a no-queue VIP pass for both of them, she hadn't even needed to mention her PR Company. It satisfied her that "The Bucks" money would go directly to women who would hate his type.

Had Greta any smarts about her she may have realised what kind of girly night this was, one look at the queue full of tactile and amorous women would have spelled out the night's clientele profile.

Greta sprinted to the VIP bar, bustling through the crowd, and plonking her bag on the counter, she didn't calm down till her chubby, ring encrusted paws were strangling a cocktail glass brimming with a very strong cosmopolitan.

The sheer unbridled excitement of the crowd was infectious and soon Greta was dancing beside her handbag, eyes closed, head thrown back sloshing cocktails in rings around her, howling along to "Dancing Queen",

Sophie spent most of the evening casually leaning against the bar, taking in the scene, casually and politely dismissing the occasional advance and invitation to dance, she wondered if the penny would ever drop with Greta as to who this night was designed for, the woman seemed oblivious, still the mood jovial. Sophie's only distraction and annoyance being Greta dancing like an idiot and bumping people.

She noticed a gorgeous looking couple of girls kissing and whispering to each other, they were immaculately dressed and utterly beautiful, the ultimate feminine "lipstick" lesbians. She bought them drinks and had the barman deliver them saying they were with Greta's compliments. Within minutes they were over chatting to her each with an arm around each other's waist.

The tribute band struck up "Chiquitita" and as if planned, the girls looked at each other and began tenderly kissing. Greta was dumbfounded and rooted to the spot, her jaw hung slack, and her eyes were wide in her head. Sophie smirked to herself, let the moment linger, and let Greta take it all gloriously in.

The girls kissing looked so glamorous, it was romantic and subtly erotic, each stroked the others hair and neck, hands moving slowly down the shoulders to the small of the back, there was no frenetic groping, it was slow, languorous and tantilising to watch. They broke from their kiss and looked deeply into each other's eyes before they realised Greta was staring at them. They giggled and walked away leaving Greta dumbstruck. "Wow" was all she could say as she drained the last of her cocktail, she was far from offended and Sophie knew she was turned on by that display; her cleavage and throat were bright pink and flushed. Fanning her flushed face with her hand made it even more obvious, it wasn't caused by her awkward dancing.

Sophie was the master at conditioning people and she knew she was sending this old gin sop home excited, curious and horny. It was one step closer to her goal.

CHAPTER 19

Her boss's attitude worried her. He was snappy, short with her, and had banged his office door more than once this week. She knew that SHE was the problem. She also knew there was trouble at home, a minor rebellion on Greta's part and the fall out was coming down squarely on her shoulders. Each evening of the previous week had been interrupted by late night text messages from the woman, diva behavior and tantrums, railing at her husband's Po faced attitude, hers was the behavior of a spoilt teenager giving two fingers to overbearing parents. The ultimate insult being, that she had entered his bedroom, looking for sexual release, to be unceremoniously turned away with the hurtful rebut of "cop on, a woman of your age should know better". Sophie couldn't have scripted his response better, but he was now taking his frustrations at home life upheaval out on her.

She had Greta nicely lined up for conquest and the time was coming to ramp up her efforts before this bastard thought of a way to dispose of HER from his office and subsequently his home life. She knew he wanted back the fucked up normality and peace of his home pre-Sophie.

His childish displays of annoyance pissed her off, he was making his grievance too obvious, and perhaps a little complaint to HR might cool his jets? That was an idea to keep on the back burner; her work was flawless so if he had a complaint with her it was solely to do with issues outside the workplace i.e. personal.

In the modern work environment his current behaviour was unacceptable, tantamount to bullying and definitely grounds for dismissal. She kept a diary logging each dirty look, slammed door, smart comment, and saved each uncomplimentary memo and email that came her direction. It was pretty damning stuff looked at in the whole; it really did portray a serious grudge or corporate bullying; that is if you didn't know how Sophie was stirring it up after hours.

She knew she must keep that line of attack until all other avenues were exhausted, it would be corporate suicide for her to make a serious and very public complaint about her boss and bring any kind of legal action into the situation, in a small city like Dublin where everyone knew everyone else, it was tantamount to making herself unemployable. It was not in her best interest.

Mr.O'Reilly's day of reckoning would come but she would control the situation herself and not leave anything to chance with outside influence or risk.

CHAPTER 20

The subject of death and decay had interested her from an early age; she held an early memory of finding a translucent pink, bald, fledgling chick that had fallen from its nest in the old sycamore tree in her back garden. It had clearly broken its neck on impact, but Sophie had scooped it up gently in her infantile chubby fingers and placed it gently in a shoebox lined with toilet paper. She ran her fingers over its cool stubbly skin, pliable little bones and distended stomach, and was fascinated by the dark bulging eyes under the paper thin skin.

The box was placed in the garden shed, and everyday that spring she checked its progress of decomposition until it finally disintegrated to a purple, bloated bag of putrid smelling mush in the bottom of the box. She had never told anyone about the chick but it ignited a curiosity rather than a fear or disgust of death.

Even though she had an extensive collection of books on serial killers there wasn't one she could identify with. They all seemed to have one or two things in common —none of which related to her.

Some were abused, had come from dysfunctional or violent homes, they had been exposed to cruelty, had overbearing mothers, had been bullied or rejected. She could lay claim to none of these experiences.

Her childhood had been no different to any other South Dublin middle class little girl; her parents were kind and not overly strict. Thankfully, she was never abused by notorious priests, neighbours with sweets in their trouser pockets or dodgy uncles.

She had vivid memories of family days out and holidays, long sunny, summer holidays from school playing hopscotch, elastics, chasing and kick the can. The play was punctuated by the ice-cream van; coppers were gathered to buy a "screwball" all for the chewing gum at the end of the cone shaped tub. Pocket money was earned, and penny sweets were shared and swapped with friends, each competing for the blackest tongue from eating "Blackjacks". Long afternoons were spent on a neighbors' low front wall, legs swinging while they sucked cool pops in the sunshine, mowers throwing out the juicy aroma of freshly cut grass. Summers of cycling around her area with those same friends, all with cardboard clipped to the front wheel with a clothes peg, the cardboard buffeting the spinning spokes, pretending they were motorbikes.

Her house always had some injured or stray animal in need of shelter and succor, her father was a softie, and applied his medical knowledge to patch up any creature that needed it, there was a constant rotation of puppies, hedgehogs and kittens, each loved, bandaged and fed by the family, each adding a memory to her childhood idyll. The only unwilling participant in the family's animal hospital efforts was as usual, her sister; Charlotte, too squeamish and selfish to have any part in their care.

Her childhood was filled with calm and happy memories of walking the long promenade in Bray. She had fond memories of savoring the delicious sting of vinegary chips, and sitting on the wall overlooking the pebble beach. Licking dripping 99's ice creams, with the amusements behind like a soundtrack. It was an idyllic childhood. She had never known fear, abuse or deprivation.

At an early age she became acutely aware that she could sense death around her and it intrigued her. She attended the all girls' convent school in Dalkey as it was in the same village as her mother's GP surgery. She would walk to the surgery after school each day and complete her homework while her mother saw the last of the day's patients.

She was friendly to everyone who came in; the regulars knew her name and some of the mothers would trust her with their toddlers while they went into the treatment room.

She could just sense though when someone was gravely ill, it was like a sixth sense, a smell that invaded her nose, and she hated it.

One day while in fifth year, she was waiting on her lift home, browsing through the well thumbed gossip and fashion mags in the waiting room when an elderly gentleman came in with his middle aged son.

The man was bowed with age on his stick, eyes red and rheumy. The sickly, sweet smell of death she experienced she had narrowed down to hyacinths', it was the closest smell in nature she could find to death. The smell clung around him like cheap perfume; she wondered why no-one else was gagging?

She forced herself to make polite conversation with him but in her head he was rotting and putrefying before her eyes. She had excused herself and vomited and dry heaved in the toilet, she was angry at her mother, why was she letting this man live like this? She had all the drugs at her disposal to end his miserable life and she was wasting the opportunity.

The portly middle aged son fussed and clucked around his father, fixing his tartan lap blanket and handing him magazines he had no interest or eyesight left to read.

Sophie noticed the son wasn't wearing a wedding ring, had most likely dedicated his prime years to looking after his father, and doing so forgoing the opportunity of a wife and family for himself. She had seen plenty like him in the surgery waiting room, fussing over elderly parents and not realising their chance at a normal life was being robbed from them, was slipping away through their unselfish and blind loyalty.

It was obvious the toll of looking after a dementia riddled and elderly parent weighed heavily on him, his face wore premature wrinkles, and his eyes were baggy and gave away the obvious signs of sleepless nights dealing with his father's nocturnal and bewildered wanderings.

A well of resentment rose in Sophie's craw towards this old man. He was wearing down his son, stalling his life and condemning him to a lifetime of loneliness, she forced herself not to glare at the old man.

The urge to rise from her seat and beat him around his wizened skull with his own walking stick was overwhelming but she fought it, digging her nails into the wooden arm rests of her chair instead.

She wanted to end the son's endless drudge and penury. She was silent all the way home in the car and snappy with her mother.

Her mother brushed it off and reasoned that exam pressure and teenage hormones were the cause of Sophie's bad mood.

For days she kept the image of the needy old man and his care worn son in her head, and frequently daydreamed about how she would kill him, she even wondered if an opportunity might arise where she could gain the sons confidence and offer to visit his father at home.

She watched the door of the surgery for weeks, each patient that filed in was a disappointment when it wasn't the old man and his son. Luckily for the old man he had been saved from Sophie's help by a placement to a local nursing home.

CHAPTER 21

Greta was now totally comfortable in her company and without any prompting she would link Sophie's arm when they were out and about, firm friends. Greta fed off Sophie's youth and energy and it played well for what was planned.

Sophie decided it was time to up the ante and make her move. It was time to give Greta a flash of the flesh —so to speak.

She booked a day spa with heated pool for them, it was a female only day and the staff assured Sophie that yes, it was ok to be naked in the steam-room or sauna that day. Perfect.

Her body was utter perfection, neither bony and thin or muscular and unattractive; she wasn't stupid enough to believe size zero was perfection. She was toned like an athlete and utterly feminine, she had to be it was her stock in trade.

She had pert full breasts and a flat stomach, her ass hadn't reached the age where it started to dip over the back of her legs, it stood proud, round and peachy. She had no cellulite; no acne marked her tanned and toned skin. She glowed with good health and she was determined to let Greta see it.

They arrived early to the spa and Sophie could see from the registration book that they were the only booking till lunchtime; the recession had definitely taken its toll on this indulgent business. They were handed fluffy snow white toweling dressing gowns, hair bands and slip ons.

In the changing room Greta turned her back to Sophie while getting undressed with the dressing gown draped over her broad shoulders for privacy. Sophie on the other hand, simply stripped off and continued talking to her as though they were in a café or shop.

She stood naked next to a full length mirror knowing Greta could see her reflection, she caught her taking a sneaky look at her naked body and it was obvious the woman was shocked at her beauty. Sophie smirked to herself as Greta's gaze lingered a little longer than was decent. "That's enough for a first sneaky peek I think" thought Sophie to herself as she drew the dressing gown around herself and tied the thick belt. She tied her hair up in a high ponytail.

Greta's facial left her red and splotchy while Sophie was radiant. They sipped coffee while their feet were pampered and pedicured. Greta's hard, calloused feet needed a lot of work, where Sophie simply needed a foot massage.

They lay side by side in the treatment room as the beauticians treated them to a massage accompanied by gentle whale song and scented candles. They lay face down and chatted easily while the girls gave them back massages, to the entire world they looked like mother and daughter have a girly day.

After much persuasion Greta agreed to try the steam-room and sauna, Sophie suggested the sauna first but after five minutes Greta wanted to escape saying the dry heat didn't agree with her smokers' chest. Sophie led the way to the steam-room with a disgruntled Greta moaning and complaining behind her despite the days pampering.

The woman was beyond ungrateful and spoilt. A healthy waft of steam escaped as Sophie gently nudged her forward and through the mist to the benches at the back of the steam room, she still had her dressing gown on and after much coaxing Greta finally parted with it to reveal a very unflattering, bold floral and old fashioned swim suit.

She sat self consciously brooding with her hands in her lap to cover the fact that her pubic hair was sprouting like spiders legs from the edges of her gaudy swimsuit. Sophie was disgusted that the basic art of feminine grooming eluded this woman.

Sophie flicked the dressing gown back off her shoulders and let it slide down her sides to reveal her perfect tits and erect nipples. She untied the belt while looking directly at Greta and let the dressing gown fall slowly to the floor, it was a basic burlesque maneuver she had learned and it was utterly erotic. She stood revealing her naked body and smooth hairless pussy bar one crisp golden curl which is exactly where Greta's eyes shot to.

The older woman was wide eyed with shock and swallowing hard, Sophie lightly sat down beside her, released her hair from the ponytail and leaned back on her elbows to enjoy the steam. Sophie knew her hair was tickling off Greta's upper arm and it would have the same erotic effect as if being brushed by a feather.

After much cajoling and banter she convinced Greta to be brave and strip off. "c'mon, live dangerously!" she encouraged her. Greta stood, turning her wide back to Sophie and wrestled the swimsuit down over her saggy arse and thick legs; she awkwardly disentangled herself from its grip and flopped down on the bench again. From the corner of her eye Sophie could see the pendulous, saggy tits hanging limp against her chest.

"There you go, just the girls together!" offered Sophie as she patted Greta's upper thigh. They shared a smile and then Greta meekly asked "Em, Sophie, have to ask, how did you manage to get rid of all the hair from, well, down there?" the innocence of the question nearly caused Sophie to laugh in her face but obviously her interest was piqued, plan B.

She turned to face Greta, locked eyes with her and took her hand, before Greta could resist or pull back her hand was cupping Sophie's pussy, she slightly opened her legs for the woman. "See? Nothing there at all, lazered away, isn't it lovely and smooth?" she stared directly and intensely into the woman's eyes, her hand was still cupping her pussy and gently kneading it. Sophie moved her hips forward ever so slightly on the bench and placed her hand over Greta's; with slight downward pressure she maneuvered Greta's finger tips between the lips of her pussy so she could feel the warm moisture. Greta swallowed hard, becoming aroused and didn't pull away, Sophie leaned towards her and gently kissed her lips, she delicately tickled Greta's lips with the tip of her tongue till she felt the older woman's mouth open to her kiss and reciprocate.

She massaged Greta's saggy tits and slid the palm of her hand over the round of her belly and down between her legs, the coarse bush of hair was scratchy and horrible to the touch but Sophie threaded her fingers through it to reach the fat fleshy lips and her clitoris. Greta opened her chubby legs to welcome her hand.

Sophie listened to her breathing, and ignored the older woman's inept fumbling at her pussy and instead concentrated on heightening Greta's arousal. She encouraged the woman's hands to clutch her ass, her tits, whatever worked – she gave her full access to her body. She was an expert in pleasure and it didn't take long before Greta was snuffling, crying, mewing like a cat and panting hard. This was the best orgasm she would ever experience in her life.

Afterwards they both lay back on the wooden benches giggling like school girls; they showered together like lovers, soaping each other's backs.

Greta smiled all the way home, even planting a big kiss on Sophie's lips before she got out of the car, The bottle blonde housekeeper held open the door and stared at Sophie, the bitch smirked and slammed the door once her employer was inside.

CHAPTER 22

The childish text messages began the next day, pleading and imploring her to meet again soon. Greta was obviously looking for a repeat performance, greedy bitch.

The next trick was to covertly film the antics now the ice had been broken, but it was down to Sophie to allow Greta make the moves and take the lead. It had to look like Greta was the dominant one, the predator.

Thankfully for Sophie a number of gadget and spy shops had opened in Dublin during the boom, cameras secreted into clock faces and even teddy bears for the paranoid parents with foreign child minders. They were inexpensive, easily concealed and for someone tech savvy like Sophie a doddle to install. She could even call in a contact she had made in a security firm if needed, he specialised in corporate surveillance, little did people know that in Ireland's largest and family owned grocery chain he had installed covert cameras in the roof tiles of the public toilets and staff changing rooms.

The cost of shoplifting and in-house theft was a much higher price to pay than possible litigation. Of course the staff and public never knew they were being secretly recorded. His discretion came at a high price.

She chose a discrete but high definition mini cam with Wi-Fi link, it could be viewed and reviewed using an app on her smart phone, it even had an edit facility in its suite of high tech settings, and of course every image was stored to a removable hard drive.

The mini-cam meant she could place it anywhere in a room of her choosing; she carried it always in her handbag, it was smaller than a lipstick. The small piece of technology was going to ensure her day job stayed on track once she had sufficient blackmail material.

The temptation to use it during one of her kills was utterly tempting – however she wasn't stupid enough to record herself committing the crime. If she wanted to re-live a situation all she had to do was close her eyes and focus and let her photographic memory do the rest. Too many killers had been caught by keeping trophies and recordings.

It wasn't long before she had footage of Greta's demands in her car, her house-while the cleaner was downstairs!, and even in the toilets of one of Dublin's top Michelin starred restaurants. All the while Sophie played the compliant submissive role, she followed Greta's increasingly demanding instructions, the sheer greed of the woman for orgasms knew no bounds.

It was draining for Sophie and she got no pleasure whatsoever from the process, but then she had her own kind of pressure release valve and stress relief.

It irked her that each time she brought Greta to orgasm the woman clung to her like a limpet, trembling and mumbling gibberish in her ear, kissing the side of her face, infuriating. She could swear she even said "I love you" after one exceptionally strong orgasm. Perfect. The one saving grace being that Sophie had insisted on her having a bikini wax as it "increased sensitivity", at least she didn't have to battle through that vile thicket anymore.

The time was coming to use the footage and end this charade, this woman's husband was making her working life a living hell, she hated drama in work but had to feign crocodile tears while leaving his office a few days previously, she made sure other staff members saw and would use it to shore up her bullying allegations if the taped indiscretions didn't give the result she wanted.

CHAPTER 23

Sarah O'Connell had caught Sophie's eye too many times, she had watched this girl from afar, holding court in nightclubs, excessively loud, swishing her brunette extensions while atop her expensive Louboutins. She was a typical Irish model, a big fish in a little pond, not Paris cat walk material, more a PR clothes horse. This girl was happy to stand at the top of Grafton street in December in a bikini if it meant being paid and having her photo published, all the while promoting some soon forgotten business venture. Sophie's company had used her on many occasions.

This bitch hogged the limelight in Dublin's nightclubs, was loud, obnoxious, held court in the best restaurants, she expected everything for free. She delighted in being mentioned in the tabloids. Sophie despised "Sarah O'Connell —top Irish model"

The girl was the epitome of everything vile and despicable in post boom Ireland. Loud, brash, spoilt, an attention seeking Celtic tiger cub; with a monster sense of entitlement and an over inflated ego.

The girl was a big fish in the little pond of celebrity Ireland. Forever fawned over by groupies and fame whore sycophants. She was a creature borne of the ill fated and short lived boom. The bust element of the cycle hadn't touched her, why would it? She surrounded herself with the spoilt rich off spring of duckers and divers, the tax savvy elite, even those under pressure and feeling the pinch of the downturn were cute enough to put everything in the wife's name, their holidays to the "Beach Club" in Marbella weren't affected. By association Sarah reaped the rewards of the pampered lifestyle and lived for free, she was far removed from the day to day suffering of her fellow citizens. Sophie would right that injustice.

Disrespectful and rude, that was Sarah in a nutshell, Sophie had watched her, everywhere she went dismissing suitors, taking free drinks without so much as a "thank you" and it irked her. She recalled words of wisdom imparted by her father when she began dating boys. "Sophie love, always remember, it takes a lot of courage for a young fella to approach a girl, if he's not your type, at least be decent, let the lad down gently, and ALWAYS say thank you". It was obvious no one ever had that conversation with the precious Sarah.

The favorite hangout for models, minor celebrities and the Dublin social elite was a tightly packed coterie of basement nightclubs, nestled in a strip of Georgian Dublin known as Leeson Street.

It was a renowned late night hangout. Some retained the dingy basement appeal of the eighties, the era when this area had its heyday. Others had gratefully sucked at the tits of corporate investment and added some class and modernity to the surroundings. Sarah O'Connell and her usual groupies could be found in the later, swilling down the complimentary booze, managers happy that they had been graced by a "celebrity". Sure, a Z lister, but an Irish celebrity nonetheless.

The ambient lighting gave a warm glow to the polished marble walls and floor of the ladies toilets, the air was heavy with expensive perfume. Cocaine swirled like dust motes in the light, the cistern tops were lightly dusted with the illegal white powder, finger smears left track through the discarded sprinklings. The Christmas party season was in full swing, and this was the kind of "snow" the party clique favoured.

Sophie sat patiently in the cubicle, checking her Facebook feed to pass the time, she had spotted Sarah earlier. She was glad this nightclub hadn't decided to employee a toilet attendant. It would have royally fucked up her plans for Sarah. She hated the idea of a monitor in the bathroom, eves dropping, ready to spray obnoxious perfume and always making eye contact looking for a tip.

Before too long the toilet door flew open and jarred against the marble clad wall, high octane giggling spilled into the tiled room, Christmas pop tunes seeping in and clicking of high heels alerted Sophie that her prey had arrived. A glassy clunk of a champagne bottle set down beside the sink heralded her arrival at the line of sinks.

Gently opening the cubicle door she slotted herself beside Sarah at the mirror, the model was too busy patting her smudged mascara to acknowledge her. The girl was drunk but she had a legendary appetite for cocaine.

The little glass vial sparkled under the lights as Sophie tapped a generous line onto the back of her hand. Wordlessly she offered it to Sarah. Her greed made it too easy, with a quick "cheers" she grabbed Sophie's hand and snuffled the white powder up her nose before reeling back to lean on the cubicle door frame behind her.

Her face gave away her panic, her eyes blinked in slow motion and she slumped backwards into the cubicle to land in a tangled mess on the floor between the cubicle wall and toilet. Sophie picked up the bottle of champagne using a tissue and placed it by her feet, tipping the last of the powder into the neck of the bottle. Blood was already trickling from the model's nose and piss was pooling around her

Louboutins shoes. "Night night" was Sophie's parting words to the dying girl as she gentle closed over the cubicle door, using a coin to slip the lock over to "occupied". Within minutes she was sipping her cocktail at the bar before grabbing a taxi in the damp December sleet.

The Sunday papers were quick to print their condolences, "The party girl who snorted heroin", "A wasted young life", "The scourge of drugs", etc etc . . . at least Sophie would never have to listen to her annoying and attention seeking bullshit in this nightclub again.

The eulogies from her "friends" made Sophie laugh; the Facebook tributes, the Irish are brilliant at being two faced and her friends excelled themselves.

Justin Mulholland had supplied the uncut heroin without question, it had cost Sophie some minor injuries from his rough sex demands but it was worth it to get rid of the particular pain in the ass, it was a fair trade off.

The irony was that Justin never connected Sophie to the models death, in fact Sarah had dated Justin for a time, it was how she came to Sophie's attention in the first place, even before her company had employed her. How ironic then, that his drugs saw her to an early grave.

He struck a handsome figure at the models funeral, set in an ancient scenic graveyard in Wicklow. His strong arms draped around the model's "friends", the hypocritical bunch over shadowed by ancient yew trees. The papers later made a point of comparing him to a young Colin Farrell.

Sophie smiled as she hung back from the funeral crowd, watching the family, genuinely upset at the loss, shuffling mournfully towards the funeral cars, then the friends and party goers, allowing them to slip past, sniffling and checking their hair and makeup before facing the press photographers outside the gate, each inwardly hoping they looked their best in impossibly high heels and over sized shades. Justin approached and slipped his arm around her waist, she turned in to him and kissed him on the lips, savoring the fact that she was wearing Sarah's expensive MAC lipstick, she had slipped it from the girl's handbag, it went in a public litter bin outside the graveyard on the way out.

CHAPTER 24

Mr. O'Reilly's demeanor was sour, snippy and cold as stone on the Monday morning, the time was coming for a showdown, the muscles clenched in his jaw and his pinched cheeks were flush with pent up frustration, she could even see his blood was high through his thinning grey hair.

This was a dangerous time, and it wouldn't take much on her part to cause an explosive row. She needed to bring this charade with Greta to an end and shore up her job security. The woman's demands were impinging on her leisure time.

Sophie knew that choosing her battleground would be crucial. If the confrontation took place in his home it wouldn't have the effect she desired, people often gird their loins on home territory so she needed to take the upper hand and pick a battleground to her advantage.

She chose Wednesday as her D-day — in the office and fuck it, she was going in all guns blazing.

Tuesday was all about laying out the groundwork for the showdown. She entered her CEO's office with a stomach full of butterflies; this was not a man to be trifled with. She had rehearsed what she was going to say, how she would stand, when to cry, everything had to be on cue.

Her CEO — Dave Duffy was a successful man in his late fifties; battle hardened and had worked his way from inner city poverty as a child to being an efficient game-changer in Irish business circles. He was often mentioned in business columns for his various successes' and savvy decisions. His well tailored suits, neat salt and pepper hair and trim physique was down to meticulous grooming and an adult lifetime spent studying various martial arts.

Hard drive in hand, and story learned like the lines of a play, she entered his Spartan office. Within the hour she was leaving — smiling and wiping crocodile tears from her face for all the staff to see. Mr.O'Reilly's fate was sealed.

The ponderous traffic on Wednesday morning didn't bother her, she was happy to delay her satisfaction, the roads were slick with sleet, Christmas tunes played incessantly on each radio station but she left the music on, her cigarette felt like a celebratory cigar as the car shuffled past the shop fronts twinkling with lights and sparkling presents and displays. She felt festive.

Even parking her car in the soul less car-park was cheering; she sat and sipped the last of her latte, savoring the warmth of the car, humming along to "wham's" "last Christmas". Her stomach rolled over in giddy anticipation of the hell that was about to be unleashed on O'Reilly.

For the effort she had put into this she wanted a healthy return, she had laid in on thick with Duffy. She had been promised the earth, moon and stars if she didn't go public or legal. "O'Reilly was going to be fucking roasted" she was promised.

For the first time in some months she looked forward to walking into her office. Today she had the upper hand to destroy O'Reilly's career and marriage to the asshole Greta.

Today was going to be a good day. Today was her day to be a "corporate psychopath".

Duffy, the CEO was impatiently lingering around O'Reilly's door when she arrived. He was passing the time making small talk with staff members but keeping his voice down so as not to alert O'Reilly to his proximity. He hadn't slept, she could tell, his mood was controlled but ready for a fight.

He placed a paternal hand on her shoulder while opening the door for her and quickly followed behind closing the door behind them.

The rumour mill was busy while the meeting took place; occasional raised voices piqued their interest. When the door eventually opened staff scattered like rats in different directions, everyone suddenly had something very important to do.

O'Reilly was first out the door, holding a cardboard box close to his chest, the photo of Greta peeping out of the top. He took the walk of shame accompanied by Duffy and the company's security guard; he kept his eyes downcast as he made his way through the now silent and frozen staff. Sophie followed as far as the office door and observed from afar. She was the only eye contact he made as he turned and stood waiting in the lift. His hate filled stare only cut off by the closing doors, they closed like a metal coffin lid on his career.

Her plan had worked beautifully. She had primed the CEO the day before, tearfully regaling him with a sordid tale of corporate bullying, being forced to service his wife to keep her job. It was damning stuff, the video evidence alone sealed his fate, O'Reilly was livid with rage on being shown the video, the screen normally used for commercial presentations to clients.

No amount of denial, tearful or otherwise, was going to save him from Sophie's allegations. Her diaries filled with damning entries of his cold demeanor, his unpleasant e-mails and memos to her did him no favours. He roared and shouted; called her every name under the sun in front of Duffy, which did nothing to help him. All the while Sophie sat sobbing into her hands, trembling with arousal and excitement. To Duffy she was paralysed with fear. It was his job as CEO to protect her from this "fucking tyrant".

It was more than enough scandal to destroy the whole company if it was leaked to the media or made it to the courts system. O'Reilly was not coming back from this, he was finished, and now it was all about damage control for Duffy. As he said himself he would do "Whatever it took to save his company".

Sophie settled behind the desk and wiggled her arse in O'Reilly's leather chair; she swiveled from side to side, running her index finger along the polished barley twist engraving on the desks edge, as she had done many times before. Duffy let himself out sheepishly, gently closing the door and breathing a sigh of relief.

The cost of her silence had come at the price of this desk – now her desk, and an elevated and permanently secure position in the company, with all the perks that entailed. She could have been a total bitch and demanded a directorship, but there was no need for overkill or extra responsibility.

The "vintage telephone" ringtone on her mobile rang and distracted her; the sleek phone vibrated and flashed its screen on the green leather inset of the desk, demanding attention. It was Greta. She hit dismiss call. The woman would have plenty to keep her occupied once her husband got home, oh! To be a fly on the wall for that marital break-up and mother of all rows. Jesus, the temptation to make one last house call to the O'Reilly's was insanely arousing, but toxic and dangerous.

A quick browse through her phone settings and Greta's number was blocked forever. She sat back into the padded chair smiling to herself, already planning a date to celebrate her achievement. She was finally finished with the bullshit. This desk was an early Christmas present. She had put in a lot of hard work so why not reward herself by fishing online? She already had in mind the internet café she would use after work to organise it. Her change of clothes and wig sat waiting in the boot of the car for just such a spur of the moment decision.

CHAPTER 25

The scruffy terrier scrambled around in the leaf litter, tail high and stiff, in ever decreasing circles, scratching and snuffling the mouldy forest floor.

Its tail began to franticly whip from side to side; the wiry little body was wound up like a coiled spring as it bounced on the spongy, mossy ground.

The female hill walker blew her breath into her cupped hands, briskly rubbed them together and stood in a cloud of her own breath in the still, frigid forest air. She picked up her metal coffee cup from a tree stump and looked around for the dog, she had seen it scamper off into the darker part of the forest; in here the tree canopy was so dense that it was like stepping into night. She pushed the wooly hat back on her forehead and squinted her weather hardened eyes, the crows feet at the corners of her eyes webbed out as she tried to see it through the dense branches. Decades of hill walking in all weathers had given her face the hardened, leather-like look of the truly dedicated outdoorswoman.

A bright yellow backpack buckle caught her eye, it was snagged on a branch a few yards into the thicket, remnants of wind shredded black canvas clung to it like shed skin.

She made her way through the tangle of branches low on the trunks of the fir trees, she had to bend in a snakelike dance to make her way through to where the dog was yapping and barking.

Her footing was unsure on the spongy leaf litter and tangled roots, the smell of forest must rising the further in she made her way, it was oppressive under the canopy, branches clawed at her clothes and hat as if trying to snare her. The dog was refusing to return despite her increasingly angry calls.

She came free of the branches into a small clearing where a tree had succumbed to the harsh winter winds. The trunk had fallen at a drunken angle, toppled sideways, allowing some air and light onto the forest floor.

It was at the upturned clump of roots that she found the dog, intent, oblivious to her shouting, scrabbling and biting at the soil in front of his face. "fecking eejet" she thought, thinking the dog was calling on ancient instincts to dig out a rabbit or badger.

He was biting, snarling and locking onto the exposed roots, thrashing them from side to side and then excavating the accumulated leaf litter and soil in musty smelling clouds behind his paws. His head was down, claws scrapping, tail erect and stiff, yapping, biting and barking like an animal possessed; she observed this exercise with marvel at his persistence, until his digging was throwing back pieces of muck encrusted bone, one after another, more pieces, some whole and almost frighteningly like human bones, the muck and detritus started to pile up behind his quivering braced back legs.

She stood transfixed watching the dog work, a sickening slide in her stomach at the realization of what she was watching, until the dogs digging unearthed a toothless, jawless skull that rolled towards her like a child's ball, coming to rest against the side of her hiking boots, the dog turned to her yapping and bouncing at her heels, she was too shocked to reward or praise him, instead she gripped the trunk of the nearest tree and vomited into the pine needles.

She franticly wiped her mouth with the back of her shaking hand and ripped at her pockets, panic stricken, beating and ripping at the pockets of her body warmer looking for her mobile phone, she dialed 911 and pleaded to god, Jesus, fucking anyone! Like the statue of liberty, holding the phone up to the sky above the clearing,, screaming for a fucking signal.

The End

EPILOGUE

Sophie's arm was aching, the baby weighed more than she expected and she'd sat in the same position for ages, praying the snuffling bundle wouldn't wake. Her sister was taking full advantage of her generosity today.

She had to get out of here, she had a date. This one would be special and she couldn't keep this lady waiting, it was time to hand the baby back with a last gentle kiss on his baby powder scented head, all the while thinking about her plans for tonight and how she'd crack the woman's skull.

The Author, Natasha White is 41, lives in Bray, County Wicklow, Ireland, with her partner, three young children, three chickens, a cat and a dog.

While coming from a motoring and banking background she has always had an unhealthy interest in serial killers and their psychology.

From a carefree childhood in South Dublin through a turbulent and abusive marriage she has drawn on memories and feelings from both experiences. What woman hasn't entertained thoughts of murder or revenge, but what is your excuse if you've never been abused? That's the question posed by this book.

This book is an insight into Ireland in post Celtic tiger days, the boom is over and certainly the country is bust. The author hoped to draw on that from personal experience, and that of many people in Ireland, although she can't lay claim to personal knowledge of murder and disposal.

Photo Credit: **John Murphy**

Lightning Source UK Ltd.
Milton Keynes UK
UKOW05f2003310714

236137UK00001B/4/P